She was imag

Her mind raced, ▮▮▮▮▮▮▮▮▮▮▮▮▮▮▮▮ her
heart told her the t▮▮▮▮▮ was penniless and
destitute she would still love him; without
knowing it she had loved him from that very
first moment when she had looked into his dark
face. What was she to do?

She would never, ever let him suspect her true
feelings for him—she would die first.

Dear Reader

As spring leads into summer, many people's thoughts turn to holidays. This is an ideal time to look out for our holiday reading pack featuring four exciting stories—all set in the beautiful British countryside. The Yorkshire moors, Scotland, the Isle of Wight and Cornwall will be the glorious backgrounds to these four wonderfully romantic tales. Let us know what you think of them, and of stories set in the UK in general. Would you like more of them, or do you prefer more exotic climates? Do tell.

The Editor

Helen Brooks lives in Northamptonshire and is married with three children. As a committed Christian, busy housewife and mother, spare time is at a premium but her hobbies include reading, swimming and walking her comical and very lovable old dog. Her long-cherished aspiration to write became a reality when she put pen to paper on reaching the age of forty, and sent the result off to Mills & Boon.

Recent titles by the same author:

DECEITFUL LOVER
THE DEVIL YOU KNOW

STONE ANGEL

BY

HELEN BROOKS

MILLS & BOON LIMITED
ETON HOUSE   18-24 PARADISE ROAD
RICHMOND   SURREY   TW9 1SR

*First published in Great Britain 1992
by Mills & Boon Limited*

© Helen Brooks 1992

*Australian copyright 1992
Philippine copyright 1992
This edition 1992*

ISBN 0 263 77609 3

*Set in Times Roman 10 on 12 pt.
01-9207-54537 C*

Made and printed in Great Britain

CHAPTER ONE

'HELL'S bells! He hasn't seen me! He's going to hit me!' Even as she gasped the words into the cold frosty air, Tania flung herself awkwardly off her bicycle, just as the wildly honking old jalopy intent on overtaking the sleek red sports car reached her. She was aware of landing in a stunned heap on the crisp white grass of the tiny verge at the same time as the back wheel of her old bike was whipped under the car's screaming tyres, drawing the rest of it along the harsh surface of the road in screeching protest. There was a high medley of squealing brakes, the caustic smell of burning rubber, and then all was breathtakingly silent for a long, still moment.

'Are you all right? Are you hurt?' As two strong arms raised her into a sitting position on the hard ground she raised dazed blue eyes to the dark face staring down at her, noticing even in her shocked stupor that she was looking at one of the most handsome men she had ever seen off the big screen.

'I don't think so.' Her voice trembled and she took a deep breath of the icy air. 'Just bruised and winded, as far as I can feel.'

'Good. Just sit still for a moment.' As the occupants of the battered old Morris ran back up the road towards them, their young faces white and distressed in the light from the street lamps, the man stood up slowly, an expression of cold anger contorting the finely chiselled features.

5

'Who was driving?' he asked the frightened teenagers grimly.

'Me.' A young lad who couldn't have been more than eighteen stepped forward, looking as though he was going to faint at any moment, his round face blanched.

'You stupid, mindless moron!' There was a slight accent clipping the furious voice as he spat the words into the boy's quivering face, and with one swift movement the man grasped the lapels of the youth's denim jacket, drawing the unfortunate boy up and towards him until his feet were leaving the floor.

'I'm going to teach you a lesson you will never forget.' The words were all the more frightening for being delivered in a low but distinct, almost conversational tone of voice that belied the savage rage twisting the dark face into a devil's mask. 'You won't mow down anyone else in a hurry.'

'Please don't.' As Tania raised herself shakily to her feet she was wryly aware that she had been almost forgotten in the drama being enacted in front of her. 'I'm not badly hurt; please don't make it worse.' She caught hold of the man's immaculate suit sleeve as she spoke, pulling nervously with all her strength, but the iron-hard-muscled arm didn't lower an inch.

'Get out of my way.' The deep voice was as cold as ice and he didn't even glance at her as he spoke.

'You touch him, mister, and we'll do for you.' One of the other lads had moved closer to the man's side, his studded leather jacket and carefully torn jeans incongruous against the fine wool suit. 'You hit him and you take us all on.'

'It will be my pleasure.' Burning black eyes flicked disdainfully over the group of boys as though they were mere children, and something in the hard gleaming gaze caused the youngsters to glance nervously at each other, seeking moral support as they shuffled hesitantly nearer.

'Please, this is ridiculous; leave him alone,' Tania begged urgently as her heart began to thud. She sensed a confrontation here of dynamic proportions. In spite of the vastly superior height and breadth of the big, broad-shouldered figure standing so calmly before the group of scowling boys, there was no way five against one balanced. 'It's nothing to do with you anyway—just mind your own business.'

'Yeah, do what she says and mind your own business,' one of the larger lads jeered blusteringly, his swaggering stance freezing suddenly as he received the full glare of the blazing black eyes.

'Shut up, Mick.' The boy still held in the vice-like grip of the man's large hands spoke abruptly. As the target directly in the firing line in this little scenario, he was clearly hoping for a peaceful conclusion, having felt the leashed power in the hands so close to his neck. 'Look, I'm really sorry. I'll get you a new bike—anything.' His scared eyes pleaded with Tania.

'That's not enough.' The icy voice was unrelenting.

'Hang on a minute.' Tania felt the hot temper that went with her chestnut hair begin to rise at the authoritative tone. 'Who are you to say it's not enough? I was the one knocked off my bike.'

'You're not sympathising with this clown, are you?' The note of incredulous amazement in the deep voice was almost comical. 'Another moment and you would have been under his wheels.'

'Well, I wasn't, was I?' Tania's soft heart had been stirred by the desperation in the boy's eyes. He looked very much like her younger brother Rob when preparing to face her father's wrath over some misdemeanour. 'I'm

OK, and he's offered to pay for the bike; what more do you want?'

The man swore softly in answer, shaking the boy slightly like a dog with a bone. 'This idiot has been trying to pass me for miles back there, and then he chooses the bend on a hill to overtake, rendering himself virtually blind, and you ask me what I want? Blood,' he finished grimly.

'Well, if he'd been trying to get past you for so long, why didn't you let him?' Tania asked sharply, her heart-shaped face flushed with a mixture of anger and fright. A small part of her couldn't believe she was having this conversation, but it seemed to be deflecting a lethal situation. Besides, there was something in the man's lordly manner that made her want to challenge such biting arrogance, make him more human.

'Are you trying to tell me this is all my fault?' The voice was like acid, but a slightly bemused expression had crept across the dark face. 'Are you insane, girl?' He looked down at her as she stood militantly before him, her slight figure lost in the thick duffel coat and fur-lined boots she was wearing as protection against the numbing cold. 'Am I the only normal person here?'

Whatever he was, he certainly wasn't normal, Tania thought irrationally. He was the stuff dreams were made of. The thick black curly hair and beautiful, heavily lashed brown eyes could have looked feminine on anyone else, but, added to the harsh, cruel, handsome face and rugged, cold features, they were heart-stoppingly sensual.

As she gazed into the tight eyes locked on hers a wave of dizziness swept over her, and as her eyes dilated he took her arm firmly, pushing the boy to one side abruptly as though he was a piece of discarded rubbish. 'I told you to sit still, didn't I?' His voice was low and furious. 'I don't know who's more stupid, you or them.'

She was concentrating with all her mind on not passing out and couldn't reply, but her bloodless lips and cloudy eyes spoke for themselves. 'Give me strength!' The steel grip on her arm lessened with the irate words, and he had bent forward and whisked her up into his arms before she realised what had happened.

'You lot stay here and don't move.' The boy he had been holding had sunk down on to the floor as soon as he had been released, his whole body shaking. He clearly wasn't going anywhere. 'I'll be back in a minute and I want names and addresses and insurance details, so get writing.'

He strode the few feet to his car in seconds, carrying her as lightly as though she were a child. She closed her eyes, not daring to look up into his cold face, horribly aware of the delicious smell emanating from his brown skin and the muscled power in the strong arms holding her so gently.

'Drink that.' After placing her carefully into the front seat and pulling a thick car rug round her trembling legs he gave her a small flask of brandy. Her hands were shaking so much that she couldn't pour the liquid into the flask top, and, taking it from her, he poured a generous measure into the silver cup and held it to her lips. 'Drink it.'

'I don't drink alcohol.'

'Drink it. You're in shock.'

'I'll be all right——'

'If you don't open your mouth and swallow this damn stuff I'll tip it down your throat.'

Her eyes were luminous with weak tears as she took a sip of the dark liquid, gasping and choking as it hit the back of her throat in burning waves.

'All of it.' His voice was relentless, and as she obediently spluttered her way through the rest of the cup he stood watching her quietly, shaking his head in disgust. 'I've never seen fine old brandy so maligned.'

He was gone before she could reply, and as she watched him talking to the teenagers through the misted car window she had to admit that the neat alcohol had brought life back to her limbs and steadied her trembling stomach. The faintness had receded, leaving in its place a feeling of strange unreality, which intensified as she glanced round the opulent interior of the gleaming car.

'Right, I'll take you home.' He had joined her as silently and swiftly as a wild animal, and she flinched nervously as he slid into the driving seat beside her, and then sat with her hands clenched in her lap, hoping he hadn't noticed the involuntary gesture. His mouth was set in a grim straight line and the austere features gave nothing away as they passed the dispirited boys clearing the road of debris from the shattered bike. It made Tania's stomach turn to see the mangled remains of her bike as they drove slowly by, and she gulped deep in her throat, fighting an overwhelming desire to lay her head on the soft leather seat and howl like a baby.

'How do you feel?' The deep voice was gentle as he glanced at her briefly in the dim light. He had clearly noticed her distress and understood the reason for it.

'I'm all right,' she replied stiffly, keeping her eyes straight ahead, petrified she was going to break down completely in front of this autocratic stranger.

He shrugged his big shoulders as he concentrated on the dark road ahead. 'It could have been a lot worse. It would have given me a great deal of satisfaction to teach those young puppies some sense.' She didn't reply, and he didn't seem to expect one.

He stopped the car out of sight of the accident and turned directly to face her, switching on the interior light on the dashboard as he did so. Her stomach jolted as she noticed again the cold dark face, his black eyes slightly narrowed as they searched her features, the sensual mouth cynically hard. She saw that a thin white scar ran across one high chiselled cheekbone, giving an air of piracy to the bronzed face.

'Where am I taking you?'

'What?' She seemed to be drowning in those glowing eyes, and for a moment his words didn't register in her brain.

'Your destination. What direction do you want to go?' His low voice was carefully patient; he clearly thought she was in shock, and so she was, but more from the impact of those piercing eyes than what had gone before.

'Oh, I'm sorry. You've got to turn round.' I sound like a stammering schoolgirl, she thought irritably, clenching weak hands together in an agony of helpless frustration. Suddenly all she wanted to do was to get home to her little rented flat and soak her aching body in a hot bath. Her knees felt sore, the palms of her hands were skinned and there was a dull throbbing in the back of her head where it had made brief contact with the hard frosty ground.

After giving him directions in a shaking voice she settled back in her seat as he started the engine, staring determinedly out of the window, willing herself to remain in control until she was alone.

As the car came to a smooth standstill outside the large old country house where Tania had her flat she was out of the door before he had time to move. 'Thank you very much indeed for all your help. I'm sorry for any inconvenience this has caused you and I hope it hasn't spoilt your evening too much.' She hurriedly spoke the words she had rehearsed parrot-fashion on the short journey home as she closed the car door.

'Hey, *bambina*! Just a minute.' The foreign voice held a thread of laughter as it arrested her halfway up the steps to the entrance porch. 'Aren't you forgetting something?'

He followed her to where she stood, wide-eyed and tawny-haired, in the harsh glare from the bright light over the big glass doors. 'I don't think so.' She stared up at him nervously, intimidated by his great height. 'I've said thank you.'

'And very graciously.' There was no doubt about it, he *was* laughing at her. Her hackles rose instantly, banishing the self-pity that had been threatening to swamp her. The quick temper that went with her dark red-chestnut hair came bubbling to the surface.

'Well, Mr Know-all? What have I forgotten?' The tart words hit home immediately, wiping the lingering amusement from his face as though by magic.

'Ungrateful little thing, aren't you?' He towered over her five feet six inches, although she had never thought of herself as short. 'Aren't you a trifle young to be such a sourpuss?'

'I'm not a sourpuss.' The words stung her to the quick. She had often prided herself on her ability to remain cheerful in the face of adversity, and there had been plenty of that lately.

'No?' The deep voice was sceptical. 'Perhaps I caught you on an off day, then?'

'Perhaps.' She glared at him, her voice clipped with anger.

He sighed heavily as though dealing with a truculent child. 'I don't know,' he said wearily, 'they let them on the roads these days before they're out of nappies.'

She had the distinct impression he was referring to her this time and not the unfortunate boys, an idea his next words confirmed.

'Why were you riding a bike with no lights, anyway? I didn't mention that at the time, for obvious reasons.'

'How very magnanimous of you,' she replied scathingly, her blue eyes shooting sparks. Just who did he think he was, anyway? 'I didn't intend to be out in the dark, as it happens, not that it's any of your business,' she finished fiercely as he clucked reprovingly in his throat.

She had no intention of explaining to him that she had been kept waiting for over two hours at the interview she had been asked to attend that afternoon, and then abruptly dismissed after a short, cursory and patently unsuccessful meeting which had bordered on an interrogation. Why did some parents think they could be as rude as they liked when seeking a nanny for their precocious offspring?

'I could get a little tired of you telling me what is my business and what is not,' he said thoughtfully, a small flame glinting in the dark depths of his eyes.

'Really? Well, as we shan't meet again after tonight, I'm sure neither of us will lose any sleep over that,' she replied cuttingly. She knew she was behaving badly and quite out of character, but his criticism on top of everything else was just too much to take.

A small muscle jerked in the square jaw as he looked at her consideringly. 'I'd like to take you over my knee and spank some sense into that perverse little head of yours.' His dark eyes lashed her angrily. 'I have the feeling you are trouble spelt with a capital T.'

She went to reply but there was something burning in the hooded eyes that caused the words to dry up in her throat with a little shiver. She stared at him wordlessly, face flushed and eyes bright.

'Here.' He thrust a piece of paper into her hand with a gesture of contempt before turning away. 'Just make sure you get the new bike fitted with suitable lights. You are a danger to yourself and everyone else, behaving so irresponsibly.'

She glanced quickly at the sprawling writing covering the paper, listing names, addresses and insurance details, annoyed with herself that she had forgotten to ask for it in the haste to escape, and scowled defiantly at his departing back. 'The accident wasn't my fault, you know!' she called into the darkness. 'If someone comes at you on the wrong side of the road there isn't much you can do about it, whether you're lit up like a Christmas tree or not.'

He had just got to his car, but spun round at the sound of her challenging voice and took the steps two at a time, reaching her in a moment. Her heart leapt into her throat at the dangerous fury jumping from his flashing eyes, he was so very big. 'You have to have the last word, don't you? If there's one thing that gets under my skin it's a pushy female. You've done nothing but argue with me all night, and I'm damned if I know why.' He took hold of her slim shoulders, moving her backwards into the soft shadows at the side of the door, his eyes narrowed in the dark, arrogant face. 'Do you like to provoke the male sex? Is that it?'

'Let me go!' She struggled slightly in his grasp, and was surprised when the light hold tightened and he moved her still further into the blackness. 'I said let me go!' She was thoroughly frightened now, and satisfaction gleamed momentarily in the cold eyes.

'It doesn't take much to tame the little wildcat, then?' His voice was slightly husky as he bent over her slight form, and when the cool hard lips brushed her face fleetingly she was transfixed with surprise for a second, the blood pounding in her ears.

'Mmm, sweet, very sweet...' he said softly against the red silk of her hair, his mouth claiming hers in more searching intimacy as she stood, dazed and pliant, in his arms. He pulled her closer into his rigid body, and as she felt a swift response in her own she kicked out blindly, suddenly panic-stricken.

'Why, you little——' He looked at her in surprise as she stood still within his grasp, flushed and panting.

'You deserved that.' The words came out on a sob of bewilderment. She was horrified to find that the seductive tang of his aftershave was sending tiny tremors of excitement coursing down her spine, amazed and ashamed at her primitive reaction to his overpowering maleness.

He looked at her silently for a long moment as she stood, small and defiant, before him, the sapphire eyes huge and frightened, daring him to disagree, but holding an unconscious plea in their soft depths.

'You're probably right,' he drawled mockingly after a time, the dark brown eyes sweeping over her flushed face and tremulous lips. 'I'd forgotten how even small pussy-cats can deliver a nasty scratch. It was worth it,

though. I haven't been tempted like that in a long time.'
His smile was cold and taunting, chilling her blood. 'You
should be very careful when you play your little games,
my dear. You might find yourself in serious trouble one
day.'

She could hear his mocking laughter as he walked
swiftly to his car, leaving her trembling and shaken with
the strange feeling that something catastrophic had happened. The cold evening air, spicy with the tang of
woodsmoke, cooled her hot face as she stood quietly in
the concealing shadows until her legs felt as though they
belonged to her again.

'What a night,' she muttered ruefully to herself as she
climbed the steep carpeted stairs to her small flat on the
top floor. 'What a rotten, stinking night.'

The persistent ringing of the telephone by her bed jerked
her from deep sleep the next morning, and as she reached
out a fumbling hand to lift the receiver every nerve in
her body twanged in protest. 'Ow!' The involuntary exclamation slipped from her lips as she picked up the
phone, and at once the harsh tones of Mrs Jenkins, her
landlady, sounded down the line.

'Miss Miles? Is that you?'

'Yes, Mrs Jenkins,' replied Tania wearily, resigned to
yet another long lecture about the overdue rent.

'I think you had better come downstairs immediately.
It would seem some flowers have been delivered for you.'
The stiff voice throbbed with disapproval.

'For me?' But the telephone had been replaced with
a firm click at the other end. She was obviously well and
truly in her landlady's bad books this morning, Tania
reflected ruefully as she hastily pulled on a pair of old

jeans and a warm jumper, looping her heavy fall of shoulder-length hair into a quick pony-tail.

The reason for Mrs Jenkins's displeasure became clear as she reached the tiny entrance lobby to the flats via the stairs. She had smelt the heavy perfume on the second landing, and as she turned the last corner the over-whelming scent of hundreds of roses confined in such a small space was shattering. Every available inch of floor was filled with basket upon basket of the rich blooms—she counted fifteen at least.

'These can't be for me,' she muttered distractedly as Mrs Jenkins drew herself up to her full height, her thin face twitching with condemnation. 'There must be some mistake.'

'The delivery boy gave a description that fitted you to a T,' said Mrs Jenkins tightly. 'There is no one else they can be for, Miss Miles. He left this,' she added coldly, handing Tania a small card in an envelope, which had clearly been opened and read.

Tania flashed her a quick glance but the woman's grim face gave nothing away. A few lines had been penned in that sprawling hand that she instantly recognised. She read the writing with a sinking heart.

To the gentle Titian-haired maiden who made last night so enjoyable. Sweet flowers for a sweet flower. I shall remember it always.

'The sarcastic swine,' Tania muttered furiously, her face flushing scarlet. She looked up at Mrs Jenkins quickly, impulsively putting a conciliatory hand on the woman's thin arm. 'It's just a joke, Mrs Jenkins. I had a disagreement with someone last night, and this is their idea of a joke.'

'I'm not completely stupid, Miss Miles.' The older woman's plain face was rigid. 'You don't spend a fortune on red roses for a joke. This is a respectable place, I would have you know. I told you when you moved in, I don't put up with no goings-on. This house has been in my husband's family for years, and just because I'm a poor widow-woman fallen on hard times it's no reason for the likes of you to take advantage of my good nature.'

Tania looked full into the thin, bony face in front of her, trying to hide the intense loathing she felt for this dried-up, spiteful old woman. Mrs Jenkins had made a great deal of money out of her lodgers during the years, ruthlessly extracting the last penny in rent even if it left the unfortunate tenant with no money for food. The rent was exorbitant, but in the small country market town in which she lived flats were at a premium, and Mrs Jenkins had not been slow to capitalise on that fact, like the true businesswoman she was.

'I'm sorry, Mrs Jenkins. It won't happen again.'

'It had better not, Miss Miles.' The angular face was fairly bristling with indignation. 'Now, can you dispose of these... objects, please?'

It took several journeys to the top of the three-storeyed house before the entrance hall was clear, and Mrs Jenkins stood in the corner the whole time, arms crossed and foxy eyes slitted.

Tania had to open all the windows in the flat, despite the chilly November day—the cloying perfume in such volume was threatening to choke her. 'Just you wait,' she muttered darkly to the tall bronzed figure in her mind as she paced the three small rooms she called home, trying to find a place for the last two baskets. 'If I ever see you again I'll tell you exactly what I think of you, sports car and all.'

She groaned as she thought about the three months' rent she owed Mrs Jenkins. The cost of these hot-house blooms would have more than covered it. 'Obviously filthy rich and nasty with it!' she said aloud as she threw the hapless flowers into the tiny bath viciously. Her usual keen sense of humour had totally deserted her for once.

After a hot reviving cup of coffee she took stock of her circumstances, trying to put all thoughts of a tall dark stranger out of her mind, which wasn't easy when even the coffee tasted slightly of roses and the flat looked like a badly run flower shop.

Since losing her job three months before, when the family she had been nanny to had moved to America, she had been unable to find another post, in spite of her excellent references. There was just one more interview today, and if that didn't work out it meant swallowing her pride and moving back to the family home in a remote part of the Lake District, at least short-term, which she had been trying at all costs to avoid. It wasn't that she didn't get on with her parents and two younger brothers, she reflected miserably; it was just that her independence had grown very precious over the last few years, and she was loath to relinquish it lightly.

'Still, Tania, old girl,' she said despondently to the snub-nosed reflection in the mirror as she applied light make-up to her eyelids later that morning, 'you might be lucky this time. If only you looked more your age.'

She looked again at the letter in front of her on the dressing-table. It had arrived a week ago in answer to her reply to the advertisement for a nanny in the local newspaper. Every time she read it she experienced a small feeling of disquiet, a niggling uncertainty whether she should follow it through, which was why she had left this interview till last.

She read the letter aloud to the interested spectator in the looking glass.

'Dear Miss Miles,
Thank you for your prompt reply to my advertisement but I regret that the original wording may have been a little misleading. There will indeed be child-care duties incorporated in the post, but ideally I am looking for someone who will be more in the realm of a Girl Friday—able to act as both secretary and personal assistant to me when the need arises as well as providing cheerful back-up to our very able nanny, as and when required. Remuneration will be generous, and should you feel you could consider this post I would be happy to meet you and——'

She sneezed violently. These flowers would send her mad if she stayed inside any longer. It was just as well it was time to leave for the hotel where the interview was being held.

She arrived at the hotel with minutes to spare, the bus having kept to schedule for once, and a cheerful red-faced barman directed her to a small alcove at one side of the large lounge after phoning her arrival through. After taking a long deep breath she opened the door in answer to the ringing 'come in' her tentative knock had called forth.

She took one step into the room and froze in horror, her expression of amazed disbelief mirrored on the incredulous face of the big dark man sitting relaxedly behind the highly varnished desk. 'You!' They spoke in unison, and as he stood up his threatening presence seemed to fill the small space; she backed out of the door blindly, sheer animal panic taking over for the second time in less than twenty-four hours.

Her nostrils caught a faint whiff of that deliciously male aftershave and, faced with the cool, powerful aura that reached out to her with insidious fingers, she was filled with the need to get away, to run, to put as much distance between herself and this enigmatic stranger as she could.

the attack; cruel in a way which she would not have realised an hour ago. Those wild brown eyes, powerful arms that reached out to her with frightening strength, the very clothes with the need being met... As much as you respond, darling, as so you...

CHAPTER TWO

'MISS MILES?' The deep sardonic voice stopped Tania halfway across the lounge, as she had known it would. She turned slowly, like a resigned prisoner being led to execution. 'It is Miss Miles?' He was standing non-chalantly in the open doorway, his face straight but the brown-black eyes filled with mocking laughter. At her. Again.

She took a deep, shuddering breath. 'It is.'

'I am Enrico Meliora. I presume you have come for the interview?' He was clearly enjoying her discomfiture, and she was immediately filled with burning rage at this giant of a man who seemed to reduce her to a quivering wreck with one glance.

'I had. I think there is very little point in the circumstances, though, don't you?' she replied stiffly, her face burning as she still stood rigidly in the middle of the room as though she had lead weights tied to her shoes.

'And what circumstances are those, Miss Miles?' The voice was soft and taunting, with an underlying cruelty she didn't understand.

He was positively hateful; she would have loved to wipe that superior smirk off his face. She summoned up all her strength and smiled sweetly, holding her head at a slight angle as she gazed, wide-eyed, at him. 'Well, after last night and all those wonderful presents you showered on me this morning I didn't think there was anything else I could do for you.' Now she had really got the attention of everyone in the room, she noted as her clear voice cut through the muted conversations around her.

The superior smirk vanished instantly, to be replaced by thin steel. 'Quite. Shall we discuss it in here?' He was across the room in one stride, taking her arm and moving her swiftly back into the small room before she realised what was happening. He thrust her forward angrily, leaning against the door as though he thought she would try to escape again.

'*Touché*, Miss Miles. I'd forgotten the rapier tongue.' She stared at him warily. There was a deep, attractive force about him which had nothing to do with his looks, an almost tangible maleness; she could practically smell it. Help, what's the matter with me? she thought as a shiver ran down her spine.

'Now, we've ascertained that you are Miss Miles and I am Signor Meliora. Shall we perhaps proceed a little further? You aren't going to bolt again?'

'I didn't bolt!' spat Tania furiously, fighting off the intimidating sexual awareness with all of her mind. He was just a man, for goodness' sake; she had seen plenty of that species before, even fancied herself in love and kissed a few in her time. She was no naïve schoolgirl, she was a mature woman of twenty-four, even if she didn't feel like one at the moment.

The remembered humiliation of the scene with Mrs Jenkins had her glaring at him as she took the seat he offered with a wave of his hand.

'Do you have to look at me like that?' he asked. 'It's hardly the most winning approach I've come across for a hopeful employee.'

'Huh!' The one word was vitriolic.

He settled back in the large easy chair behind the desk, crossing his arms behind his head comfortably, the snowy whiteness of his shirt throwing the tanned darkness of his skin and the heavily lashed black eyes into fierce prominence. 'You don't like me much, do you?' he asked conversationally, no laughter now in the slightly cruel face.

'No,' replied Tania shortly, standing up again, assuming that the interview was at an end.

'Sit down, Miss Miles,' he barked harshly, straightening abruptly in the chair. She sat. 'If you stand up once more before I tell you this interview is at an end I'll tie you to that damned chair.' His eyes were as cold as ice, and she shivered suddenly, in spite of the central heating.

'This is all ridiculous,' she muttered defiantly, and he flashed her a cutting glance of pure frustration.

'You'd try the patience of a saint, young lady.' He lowered his eyes to the paper in front of him on the desk, which she recognised as her letter to him. Painful seconds ticked by and still he didn't speak. She heard a dog bark in the distance, and somewhere a child squealed shrilly; then all was silent again.

'I really can't believe you are twenty-four.' She glanced up at him, startled to find the slumbrous eyes tight on her face. 'I thought last night you couldn't have been more than eighteen.'

'Well, you can't always be right, can you?' Now, why did she have to say that? Tania thought miserably; her tongue had a life of its own round this man.

'Is it me in particular you have an aversion to, or men in general?' he drawled slowly, a slight inflexion on the words giving them a subtle double meaning.

'How dare you?' Tania went to stand up and then remembered the promised threat. There was something gleaming in the stony slate eyes that told her he would have no compunction in carrying it out if she defied him.

'I do like men,' she affirmed weakly, sinking back into the soft leather seat. 'Not that it's any of your...' She stopped again. The dark eyes flared briefly.

'Any of my business?' he finished frostily. 'You know, you are really quite amazing.' He leant forward suddenly, large brown hands spread out on the smooth surface of the desk. 'You arrange to come for an interview, you use up my valuable time with a series of impertinent remarks, and then you tell me I am supposed to leave the choice of questions to you? Is that it?' He swore softly in his native Italian.

'No, of course I don't expect that.' This was getting worse. 'It's just that...' She stopped again.

'Yes?' The icy voice was hardly encouraging.

'It's just that you're so...smug.' The probing black eyes opened wide with surprise, and for a heart-stopping moment Tania thought he was going to leap over the desk.

'I'm what?'

'Smug.' She wasn't going to back down now. He swung his chair round to stare out of the window, his broad back taut and rigid. An excruciating few seconds ticked by, and a little knot of apprehension tightened in her throat. The bright artificial light was glinting on the blue-black head, and she could just see where tiny gleaming hairs on his muscled neck curled down into his shirt collar... She forced her eyes away, shocked by the treacherous response in her lower stomach, and furtively wiped damp hands on the rough tweed of her skirt.

The sheer power of this man was lethal. She should have followed her first instinct and just kept walking.

'We'll go on.' She gritted her teeth as he spoke, and lifted her clear eyes to his inscrutable gaze as the chair swung round again. 'I would like to confirm a few things from your letter if I may.'

She stared at him in bewilderment. The calm, impassive face was relaxed and cool as he held her eyes with his own; it was as though the last few minutes had never happened.

'You state you are twenty-four years of age, unmarried and with no attachments. You have been seriously involved in the past, perhaps? *Un'amante*? *Degl'amori*?' She didn't understand Italian but got the gist of what he was asking, and her colour rose swiftly. He held up a placating hand. 'I need to know if there is a possibility of an estranged lover turning up on my doorstep. You are an attractive woman.'

Her eyes shot venom. 'I've had the odd boyfriend in the past, but nothing serious—my work has been too demanding. There is no question of anyone turning up on your doorstep, and you stated in your advertisement it wasn't necessary to live in anyway. I have my own flat.'

'Ah, yes.' His voice was smooth. 'It was stated that it wasn't essential to live in but would be preferred, I think?' She glared at him silently, and he continued after a slight pause, 'You spent two years at college after leaving school at eighteen with excellent qualifications, and obtained further certificates in child-care. Correct so far?'

She nodded wearily. What was the point of this farce? He obviously wouldn't offer her the job.

'After three years in a children's home I see you changed to the private sector as a nanny. Why was this?'

She looked at the cold, cynical face across the desk. How could she explain to this stranger the pain and anguish that had led her eventually to that heart-breaking decision? How could she tell him she had been guilty of the cardinal sin of getting too fond of one particular child? The thrill when Melanie had been taken away by prospective adoptive parents, the desperation when they had brought her back five weeks later, crushed and upset and pathetically at a loss to understand why her new 'Mummy and Daddy' didn't want her any more. The overwhelming shock a few months later after returning to work after a long weekend to find Melanie gone again to a different home. No, she couldn't bare her soul to this arctic mind.

'I wanted a change,' she answered briefly, raising her small chin in unconscious challenge, and the ebony eyes, watching her every move, took in the shadow that brushed her face fleetingly. He shifted restlessly in his seat and then shrugged dismissively.

'You were with the Brown family for nine months? Why was it that you didn't go to America with them? I understand from their letter of reference that you were given the opportunity.'

She had dreaded this question at each consecutive interview, for whatever reply she gave either made her look condemningly ungrateful or pitifully unambitious. She squared her shoulders and decided to tell the whole truth this time; she had nothing to lose anyway—she would imagine she was the last person on earth he would want to employ.

'It wouldn't have been the best thing for any of us,' she said quietly. 'The Browns were a lovely family, but with Mrs Brown working extremely long hours out of the home and Mr Brown having a lot of spare time on his hands . . . well . . .' she paused, at a loss as to how to continue ' . . . he seemed to be getting too fond of me. It was becoming difficult . . .'

He nodded, holding up an imperious hand as she stumbled to a halt. 'I see. You need explain no further. I thought it may be something like that. You are to be commended. A lot of girls would have taken the chance to travel and hang the consequences.'

'Not the girls I know.'

The intensity of that piercing gaze unnerved her slightly. 'Then you are more fortunate than I in your choice of female company.' He stood up, tilting his dark head to one side slightly and thrusting his hands deep into the pockets of his beautifully tailored trousers.

He moved round the desk to where she sat as Tania tried to conceal her growing agitation at his close proximity, pausing to sit on the edge, with his long legs outstretched close to her small feet. 'Now I think it is my turn to tell you something about myself and the household in which you would work.'

Her stomach muscles did somersaults as he looked down at her, but his face was remote and withdrawn. 'Owing to a business deal with a large British company, it has become necessary for me to spend a few months of each year in your country, perhaps no more than three or four, but it is not possible to be specific. I prefer to have my children with me at this stage in their lives, and therefore I have bought a house on the outskirts of this town. Great Oaks, I think it is called?'

Tania nodded. 'Yes, I know Great Oaks. It's a beautiful house.' She remembered hearing in the local post office that the Darlington family had been thrilled with the offer made by an Italian millionaire for their magnificent old house set in its own grounds. The whole village had been waiting with bated breath for the first sight of him. Surely this couldn't be...?

'One of my English friends has helped with the formalities, a Miss Selina Matheton. You perhaps know her?'

Tania shook her head as her lip curled slightly. She might have known his 'friend' would be a woman.

'Selina was going to act as part-time secretary and assistant to me while I was here, although most of the real work will be completed in my offices in Italy. Unfortunately it doesn't seem to be working out too well.'

'Mixing business and pleasure rarely does,' Tania remarked acidly, a mental picture of a long-legged expensive blonde jumping unfairly into her mind. His friend might be old and ugly!

'Quite.' His eyes narrowed and the cold face hardened fractionally at her comment. 'You did say in your letter that you could type?'

'Yes, I can, but——'

He continued as though she hadn't spoken. 'I have employed English staff to run the house for me apart from the children's nanny, who obviously accompanies them wherever they go. The children are finding it hard to settle, and tempers all round are getting a little frayed.' The dark eyes didn't leave her face for a moment. 'That is where you would come in.'

'I would?' asked Tania doubtfully.

'Apart from helping me, your other duties would be to provide some relief for Gilda as and when needed. She is an excellent nanny, but the children are far more constrained here than at home. They are used to much

freedom in Italy, and your weather, it is so inhospitable.'
He paused. 'You understand?'

She nodded slowly. 'Are you saying this post is only
for the next few months, then?'

He slapped his hand to the side of his head Latin-
style. '*Io sono stupido.*' He saw her look of surprise and
smiled gently, the smile transforming the stern face so
completely that she felt her heart leap into her throat.
'I apologise. I do not explain myself sufficiently. You
would accompany us to Italy when we return—I want
the children to know you as a part of the family. It is
important they have consistency in their lives. Then when
we come here each year, for however long it proves
necessary, they are more at home.'

'But my flat?' She glanced at him bewilderedly.

'It would be better if you came to live at Great Oaks,
but if you preferred to keep your flat all financial com-
mitments would be taken care of. That need not be a
consideration.' He spoke as though paying the rent for
an empty flat for nine months of the year was totally
incidental.

'I see.' Her mind was racing furiously, and as she
looked up at him again she surprised a curious expression in the dark face, a waiting she couldn't quite
discern. 'Is your wife in Italy?' she asked hesitantly, and
saw the firm, strong mouth tighten ominously.

'My wife died two years ago when my son was born.'
The stark words were emotionless; he could have been
discussing the weather forecast.

'Oh, I'm sorry.' Tania looked full into the expressionless face gazing down at her. He reminded her
of someone, someone she couldn't quite place . . . an unsettling person. Oh, yes, she had it now. On a recent
day trip to France she had gone to an exhibition with

some friends and been arrested by an exquisite sculpture
of a full-size stone angel. She had stood for fifteen
minutes or so before it while the rest of her party had
wandered round, captivated by the cold beauty in the
still carved face and the male grace and majesty in the
smooth, lovingly formed limbs. This man could have
posed for the sculpture, it was so like him, but the very
element that was so beguiling in cold stone was terri-
fyingly chilling in a human face.

'How old are your other children?' she asked at last
when he still didn't speak.

'My daughter is nearly four.' The words were impatient. 'When can you start?'

'What?' She stared at him uncomprehendingly.

'I said, when can you start? You haven't been offered
another position?'

'No, but...' She stammered to a halt as she met the
full force of the arrogant eyes. 'I don't think——'

'How long have you been out of work? Three months?
I should imagine your savings are somewhat diminished.'

'They are, but——'

'Well, then.' He spoke as though it were all settled,
and Tania knew a moment of stomach-twisting panic.
She had never dreamt he would offer her the job. She
couldn't work for this haughty, overbearing man,
although she knew she was mad to turn down such an
incredible offer. She just knew that if she accepted the
job the results would be devastating. His life-force was
a live entity in itself; it would suck her into his sphere
and then discard her without a moment's thought when
she was of no more use.

'I'm sorry, Mr Meliora, but it wouldn't work,' Tania
said quickly, trying to instil a note of firmness in her
wobbly voice. 'I haven't trained as a secretary or any-

thing; there must be hundreds of people who would be far better suited than——'

He interrupted her again, his voice definitely irritable now. 'Of course it would work—you are perfect for my needs.'

She stared at him with wide eyes, the subtle sensual odour of his bronzed skin filling her nostrils as he leant down close to her so his dark face was on a line with her head. The thin silver scar stood out sharply against the tanned cheek as the light caught it in its bright glare, and for a crazy moment she almost put out her hand to trace its winding path. The impulse made her catch her breath suddenly, turning her sapphire eyes liquid.

'It would be perfect,' he repeated in a soft growl. 'You don't like me, right?' His black eyes dared her to deny it.

'That's an asset?' she asked with a little catch in her voice, and he laughed mockingly deep in his throat.

'Oh, it is; believe me, my pure little English maiden, it is. Unfortunately in this wonderful world in which we live more people are driven by avarice and greed than by any other motive.' She stared at him with shocked eyes and he laughed again, coldly and without humour. 'You don't believe me? Well, I've been around a little longer than you, my sweet *bambino*, and I know how to recognise trouble a mile off. I had had five secretaries in almost as many months in Italy before my present one, Filomena, came on the scene. They all contracted a ridiculous infatuation for me within days of their arrival, causing unnecessary and time-consuming complications all round.' He made it sound as though the unfortunate women had all been suffering from an infectious disease, she thought in bemused silence.

'And Filomena?'

'Filomena is nearly sixty,' he answered grimly without a shred of humour in his voice. 'She knows that to declare herself in love with me would be quite ridiculous and totally unbelievable, and therefore she does the job she is employed to do and does it well, without any dreams of a life of luxury interfering with our work relationship.'

Tania looked at him horrified. 'Are you saying that all those girls only wanted you for your money?'

'Those and many others.' His voice was without conceit. 'I have no illusions as to where my attraction lies, Miss Miles. It has proved a valuable lesson in the school of life.' She thought he was doing himself and some of those women a grave injustice, but had no intention of voicing her opinion.

'You don't like me? Well, that's fine. You don't have to. In fact, I would prefer you not to. All I want to do is to have a contented household both here and in Italy, without any *problema romantico*. You understand?'

She tilted her small heart-shaped face slightly, her eyes showing her astonishment.

'I will make every allowance for your feelings, and recompense will be generous for your ordeal.'

She glanced at him sharply—there had been a slight inflexion in the cool foreign voice that suggested he wasn't as pleased with her opinion of him as he appeared, but he stood up slowly to move back behind the desk again, his face hidden from her gaze. As he did so, just for a moment, his muscled thigh brushed against her shoulder, fanning the soft, glowing hair across her flushed face. It was as though she had been touched by a live wire, and she jolted painfully, the cuts and bruises from the night before springing into play. He had clearly felt nothing; his face was harsh and austere as he sat back in the chair, waiting for her answer.

'Well?'

'I'm sorry to have wasted your time.' Her voice was anxious. 'This just isn't what I'd thought. In spite of what you've said, I couldn't work for anyone I didn't get on with.'

'Who said we wouldn't get on?' His eyes were like steel. 'You can dislike someone and still have a perfectly satisfactory working relationship with them. The situation seems tailor-made for my needs.'

The sheer audacity of the man was overpowering. He was totally ignoring the impossible position he was placing her in. The annoyance and apprehension she had been feeling for the last few minutes flowered rapidly into full-blown rage, and it took all her considerable willpower to answer calmly. 'I'm sorry, Mr Meliora, but I don't think I've made myself clear. I am not the person you are looking for.'

'On the contrary.' Something she couldn't quite understand flashed across the autocratic face, and then he stood up abruptly, his voice gruff. 'We will consider the matter closed for the moment. We will have lunch.' She stared at him, aghast, and he smiled mockingly, although there was no warmth in his eyes. 'You do eat, I take it?'

'Yes, but I... It's late and...' She was floundering and they both knew it.

'Just lunch, Miss Miles, and then you will be free to go?' She had noticed that his excellent English placed a question mark at the end of some of his words, but this time she felt it was meant. He was the most unsettling man she had ever met.

And certainly the most attractive. The number of female heads that swung round for a second and third look as they crossed the hotel lounge to the dining-room would have made her smile in different circumstances. She could almost read their minds. What on earth is a hunk like that doing with her? They had a point—she didn't know either.

Once they were seated at a quiet little table he leant back in his chair with a small sigh, his eyes tight on her wary face. 'I don't usually have to force someone to have lunch with me. Quite a novel experience.'

'I'm so glad to oblige.' She couldn't keep the tartness out of her voice. 'According to you, you don't have many of those.'

'What a beautiful pussy-cat you are with those huge blue eyes and red hair. It's a pity your claws are so sharp.' She could tell he was enjoying her discomfiture. 'You need taking in hand. Some regular petting and fondling would work wonders on that ruffled fur.' The mental image the softly suggestive words conjured up stained her cheeks with vivid colour, and he chuckled deeply in his throat, his eyes wicked. 'What's the matter with the boys round here anyway? Why haven't you been snapped up before this?'

She looked at him quickly to see if there was any cruelty in the dark face, but only genuine enquiry showed as he let his eyes wander over her face feature by feature. His eyes lingered on the wide full mouth, and she felt a tingling in her lips, gulping deep in her throat and unconsciously rubbing their softness as though to erase something. The glowing black eyes caught the gesture, and something flared briefly in their glittering depths before he turned away to give their order to the young waitress hovering at his side.

'What made you buy a house in this part of the country?' she asked once the waitress had gone, and he accepted the change of conversation with a slight Latin tilt to his head.

'Because it's beautiful, and I like beautiful things,' he said slowly, his deep voice stroking her nerves into a thousand tiny explosions. 'Selina had assured me the Yorkshire Dales were tranquil, and my children will benefit from that. I shall need to visit London periodically, but I wanted our base to be friendly and safe.'

'Safe?' She looked at him in surprise and met the full gleam of his sardonic gaze.

'Are you really so naïve, Miss Miles? I am a very wealthy man, and that places certain restrictions on my family.'

'Do you mean kidnapping, that sort of thing?' Her voice was horrified.

'Yes, that is exactly what I mean.' His eyes looked inward. 'My son was kidnapped when he was just a few months old. Fortunately one of the people involved got cold feet and we recovered him within hours. It was a harrowing experience.' He looked at her shocked face with cold amusement.

'What happened to them?' Her voice was a whisper.

'They won't repeat their mistake twice.' The voice was molten steel.

'You don't mean...?' She stared at him, terror-stricken.

'No, I don't mean!' His voice was proud and scornful. 'Let's just say they escaped with their lives but it will be a long time before they would think of harming a member of my family again. You don't approve?' he continued as he saw the revulsion in her wide eyes.

She shook her head slowly. 'You should have let the police deal——'

He interrupted her viciously, his eyes blazing. 'The police do their job, no more, no less. God has entrusted the members of my family into my care, and I will protect them in whatever way I have to. My method of dealing with the kidnappers let others know that retribution would be swift and sure. It has served as a necessary and apt warning. Those people would have harmed my son if it had suited their purpose. I think they got off lightly. They are still alive.'

She was immensely grateful when lunch was served, although the preceding conversation seemed to have robbed her of her normally healthy appetite.

He alluded to it once more as they finished coffee, his eyes watching her every expression. 'There would be nothing to fear if you accepted the post, Miss Miles. That sort of thing only happens once in a lifetime, and the appropriate action was taken.'

'Yes, of course.' She looked at him hesitantly. 'It's not that.'

'You are frightened of me?' His face was tight and unsmiling, and as her eyes flicked over him she saw a small muscle jerk in the tanned cheek.

'No,' she lied quickly, and he smiled that smile that didn't reach his eyes.

'You disappoint me, Miss Miles. I expect the truth from you.' His voice was warmer as he took in her flushed face. 'There is no need to fear me; I would not do anything to hurt you. If you accepted the post you would come under my protection and care, and until you resigned I would consider myself responsible for your well-being. Does that reassure you?'

It didn't—quite the opposite—but she nodded wanly, feeling for all the world like a small white moth that was being driven to seek the bright-burning light that would eventually consume it.

'Think it over.' He wrote a cheque for the attentive waitress and turned to Tania again, his face bland. 'I will take you home.' There was no invitation in the words.

'It's all right, thank you. I've made my own arrangements,' she prevaricated quickly as he rose to pull back her chair.

'The new bike has been delivered already?' His voice was caustic.

'No, of course not,' she replied, blushing furiously. 'I came by bus, as it happens.'

'By bus?' He sounded as though he had never heard of this phenomenon, and, remembering the sleek Ferrari, Tania didn't doubt why. A little flame of anger stirred in her chest.

'Yes, it's a big thing with four wheels.' Oh, help, she thought miserably as his face tightened menacingly, why can't I keep my big mouth shut? He was clearly of the same opinion.

'Quite. Nevertheless, I will take you home.' The voice was implacable.

'I thought you'd have other applicants to see?' The excuse was weak, and he smiled slowly.

'As it happens, you are the last.' He took her elbow in his hand as they left the restaurant, and she willed herself not to jerk away, his touch setting the fire alarm off all over her body.

The day had transformed itself in the last two hours as only English weather could. Instead of the misty drizzle she had arrived in, bright golden sunlight was flooding the tree-lined avenue and rolling meadows outside the hotel, lighting up the few remaining red and yellow leaves on the bare trees and turning the air crystal-clear. She saw his car immediately. It stood out from its companions in the small car park like a prince among paupers.

'You haven't mentioned the flowers,' he said smoothly as she slid into the cream leather seat. He shut the door before she could reply, walking round lazily to the driver's side, giving her time to bristle in discomfort. 'I take it from your earlier comment you did receive them?' he asked as the quiet engine purred immediately into life.

'Yes, I certainly got them,' she affirmed acidly.

'You don't sound very pleased.' The drawling voice was faintly reproving. She glanced at him in unconcealed amazement, surprise and anger warring for supremacy on her flushed face.

'What do you expect? You didn't send them for me to be pleased with them, did you?'

'I didn't?' His voice was flat. 'Why do you think I sent them, then?'

'Oh, I'm not arguing with you,' she said weakly, not fooled by the suave tone for a minute. She would only come off worse in a battle of words. 'They nearly cost me my home, as it happens.' A slight exaggeration, but she felt the circumstances called for a little embellishment.

'I don't understand. Explain, please.' He suddenly sounded very Italian.

'My landlady read your card and thought that I'd...that we had ... Oh, for goodness' sake, you know what I'm trying to say,' she said, flustered at his expressionless face as he concentrated on the winding country road.

He turned the car into a convenient gateway suddenly, driving just inside the small newly churned field so that they were all but hidden from the road, looking out on to the brown-red earth and the darker meadows and dry-stone walls beyond.

'Do you mean to tell me this woman threatened you over receiving a bunch of flowers?' he asked coldly as he turned to her with magnificent disregard for the out-rageous understatement.

'Well, it wasn't exactly one bunch, was it?' Tania re-turned sharply. 'And your card was, well . . . suggestive. She does have a point,' she added as he went to speak. 'I already owe her three months' rent and, to have such an extravagant gift, I suppose she thought——'

'It's perfectly clear what she thought.' The voice was icy. 'She had no right to read the card in the first place, and then to jump to such an assumption! Have you given her any cause in the past for such an insulting conjecture?'

Tania reared up furiously like a small tigress, her blue eyes flashing sparks and a deep red flush staining her pale cheeks. 'No, I certainly haven't,' she hissed angrily, beside herself with rage and incensed at his cool superior stance as he lay back in his seat, watching her through narrowed eyes. 'Not, I hasten to add that it's any of your——'

'Not again.' He closed his eyes briefly. 'Don't say it again. I get the message. You are as pure as the driven snow and untouched by human hands.'

He was doing it again, twisting her words to make her look foolish. 'I didn't say I lived like a nun.'

'I wouldn't have believed you if you had, not with that hair and those eyes.' He lifted a lock of soft, silky hair as he spoke, letting it run slowly through his long brown fingers, the golden sunlight through the car windows turning it dark amber in his hands. 'Exquisite, quite exquisite.' He was speaking more to himself than her, and she felt a nervous trembling in the pit of her stomach as the intimacy of their surroundings crowded in on her.

He followed the line of her slender neck up to one soft cheek as the last gleaming strand of hair slipped back on to her shoulders. 'Real English peaches and cream.' His touch was amazingly sensitive, his fingers delicate on her face, and to her horror she could feel her limbs beginning to melt in response, a dull throbbing tightening her lower stomach as he moved closer across his seat.

She looked at him with wide frightened eyes, hating the spark of excitement that was constricting her breathing and rendering her vulnerable to his burning gaze. He was so near that she could see the tiny black hairs under his skin on the hard jaw, the long thick eyelashes shading the piercing eyes. She stared at him, mesmerised, like a tiny baby rabbit caught in the harsh, glaring headlights of an oncoming car.

'Such a wild, prickly little thing,' he murmured, his voice thick and deep, his hands reaching out to hold her shoulders gently as his mouth took hers in a warm experimental kiss. She couldn't have moved if she had wanted to; his touch was letting loose a thousand small signals to her senses, sending a flood of emotion running over her like red-hot wires.

The slow kiss deepened and held, his probing tongue invading the soft sweetness of her mouth with masterful ease, causing an uncontrollable melting of her will that had her shivering against his hard chest as she fell against him with a little lost moan. She had never dreamt that a kiss could be like this.

The deliberate assault on her senses continued, his firm mouth sensuously coaxing, first dominant then gently retreating, until she was lost in a mounting vortex of desire, dazed by the swiftness of her capitulation. *'Bella, bella.'* His voice was warm against her lowered lashes and wildly flushed cheeks, his breath fanning her face as he dropped feather-light tiny kisses over her ears and throat.

She trembled helplessly and he pulled her closer to him, his breath shuddering in his throat as he leant over her, pushing her further down into the cushioned seat, his broad back shutting out the sunlight. She felt her fingers lock behind the muscled neck, and as they touched the crisp short hair he sighed deep in his chest before his mouth plundered hers again, this time fiercely eager.

'No!' As his hands slid from her shoulders down her body to the warm curves beneath she wrenched herself free, twisting in her seat so that she moved from beneath him to sit with her back against the door, her eyes wide with shock. For a second he was perfectly still, and then he leaned back into his own seat with a swift glance at her frightened face.

'And they told me the English are reserved.' The derisive mockery in the dry foreign voice cut through the daze she was in like a cold shower. She stared at him with hurt, embarrassed eyes, not noticing that his hands were shaking slightly as he rested them on the wheel and his own breathing was laboured.

She was out of the car before he could stir, almost falling into the ditch in her haste to escape.

'Tania!'

Through the buzzing in her ears she vaguely heard his angry voice, but she was running as fast as she could up the country lane, blind and deaf to her surroundings, consumed with the need to get away from this dark stranger, stumbling and sobbing as humiliation and shock put wings on her feet.

CHAPTER THREE

'WHAT the hell do you think you are doing?' Enrico Meliora caught Tania's arm, swinging her round so violently that they both nearly fell and she was forced to cling on to him for support. 'You little fool, you could have killed yourself running in the middle of the road like that!'

She looked at him, her face white in the sunlight and a trail of tears silver on her cheeks. His face softened and he shook her slightly, his expression rueful. 'I'm not a monster, that you have to run from me like that. I wouldn't have done anything to hurt you.'

A shiver shook her slight body and he pulled her into the crook of his arm as they walked back down the road towards the hidden car. He stopped again, taking a large, crisp white handkerchief from his pocket and dabbing her face gently. The unexpected tenderness brought tears pricking the backs of her eyes, and she blinked them away furiously.

'Come on, little one, it wasn't so bad, was it?' His voice was soft and faintly quizzical, and she shook her head, lowering her face so the soft hair swung across to hide her expression.

'It was just...' She stopped, confused.

'Yes?'

'I thought you thought that I was...that I had encouraged...' She couldn't go on. It was too embarrassing.

'*Scusami*, I apologise, little one.' His voice was quiet. 'The women I am used to mixing with...' He hesitated.

44

'They are more experienced at twenty-four; they would not have taken offence at my words. They were not meant to hurt you, more to put you at your ease.'

She looked at him out of the corners of her eyes, noticing the concern in his hard face. 'I see.' A small smile touched her mouth. 'I don't think you quite got it right.'

Suddenly they were both laughing together, and as she saw his austere face relax it felt as though an iron fist had reached out to grasp her heart, and her laughter died in her throat. He took her hand to lead her back to the car, and she winced slightly as his warm flesh enclosed hers; there was something about him that made her feel completely subjugated and painfully feminine.

'Come,' he said easily, 'we must get you home. There is someone waiting for you?'

She shook her head without looking up, and they walked back to the car in silence, the air cool on her hot face.

He caught the change in her eyes as they slid back into their seats and touched her hand fleetingly before starting the engine. She jerked away before she could stop herself and his expression hardened, his face suddenly tight and unsmiling. 'I'm not going to rape you, you know. I have never taken a woman by force in my life, and I've no intention of starting with you.'

She shrugged, unable to reply, and pretended an interest in the scenery flashing past the window, and after another swift glance he said no more, concentrating with grim determination on the road ahead, the leashed power of his big body intimidatingly close.

She breathed a sigh of relief as the Ferrari purred to a halt outside the house, unconsciously straightening her hands, which had been clasped in tight fists on her lap, and getting out quickly.

'I will be in touch tomorrow for your decision.' His voice was all ice again. 'I don't recall we mentioned your salary.' He named a figure that made her eyes widen as he got out of the car and moved to stand by her side.

'I can tell you my decision now.' She went to put a hand on to his arm as he moved to leave but froze halfway to touching him, the memory of their intimate kiss too vivid for her to voluntarily make contact with that hard flesh. He noticed the gesture and for a moment a red-hot flame glowed in the dark eyes, but then was banked down ruthlessly as he stared proudly into her sapphire gaze.

'I said I will contact you tomorrow.' He towered over her, his face closed. 'I can assure you that if you decide to accept the position nothing like this afternoon will ever happen again. It was a regrettable mistake and entirely my fault, one of those odd moments that get out of hand.'

She nodded doubtfully. There was no way on earth she would ever work for this man; she never wanted to see him again, let alone confer with him day after day. He seemed to sense her thoughts, and the cold eyes became jet-black slits.

'Take care that you don't miss all the chances life puts your way, Miss Miles. You'll grow into a very bitter, discontented old lady if you do. You are still young enough to make your own destiny if you have the courage to do so.' His voice was scathing.

She glared back at him, feeling less vulnerable now that she had left the close confines of his car. 'I'm perfectly capable of looking after myself, thank you. Just because I don't see the situation the way you do you needn't think you can bulldoze me into doing what you want. If that's how you are with your employees I'm glad I'm not one of them.'

'I hope I am not quite so indelicate as you would seem to suggest,' he said tightly, a look of murderous rage burning in his eyes. 'Perhaps it would be better if we parted company now once and for all, Miss Miles. There is no place in my household for a shrew.'

She stared at him defiantly, biting her lips with small white teeth, forcing back the words that were hovering in her mind. It was better just to let him go.

He eyed her speculatively. 'Not speechless at last?' He smiled smoothly, looking down into the deep blue of her thickly lashed eyes. 'Come, come, my sharp-stemmed English rose, I'm sure there is a retort burning on those soft lips?'

She remained silent as he grasped her arms with iron hands, nervously conscious of the bunched muscles in his wide shoulders, the strong, well-developed chest.

'No?' he asked as she still didn't speak. 'Then perhaps it would be better for me to give you something to remember me by.'

As she felt his hard lips come down on hers in a punishing kiss she began to struggle against the rigid body pressed close to hers, trying frantically to break herself free from his inflexible hold. It was like trying to fight solid rock.

His cruel mouth increased its savage pressure on hers, opening her lips and rifling the softness within. There was no tenderness in the kiss as before; it was meant as brutal punishment for her defiance. After a few seconds of fighting him she was alarmed to feel the same response she had felt before slowly invading her senses, and found she was struggling against herself now as much

as him, self-disgust catching the breath in her throat into
a sob.

He seemed to sense her reaction, his mouth suddenly
becoming softly coaxing as he crushed her closer to him,
a small shudder running through the large, taut frame
that found an echo in her trembling body. At last she
gave herself up to the ecstasy of the moment, but immediately she did so he moved sharply away, relin-
quishing his grip on her so abruptly that she almost fell
at his feet.

He stood, looking down at her scornfully, a hard
mocking gleam in his eyes. 'You would not defy me for
long, my good little girl. You are not so very different
from all the rest.'

She didn't stop to think. Her hand shot out as though
it had a will of its own, hitting him full across one tanned
hard cheek. He stood as though carved in stone, the only
sound in the sudden breathtaking stillness her harsh,
ragged panting. She wasn't sorry; whatever he did to her
it was worth it, she thought wildly as her hand-print
began to glow red on the dark face.

'I hate you.' She hadn't realised she had spoken the
words out loud until she heard the sound of her own
voice with a start of surprise. 'I really hate you.'

There was a strange brilliant glitter in his eyes as he
looked down at her small stiff figure, and she saw his
hands were clenched into tight fists in his pockets as
though to restrain them from reaching out. 'Do you?'
His calm voice was at odds with the blazing eyes. 'Well,
it would seem we both have something to remember from
our brief but most productive acquaintance.'

She heard the car roar away as she walked shakily up
the crumbling stone steps to the house, and turned to
watch it as it flashed scarlet among the bare trees and

bushes lining the winding country lane. It disappeared from her sight at a bend in the road, the expensive tyres screeching protestingly, and gradually the sound of the engine died away until the quiet of the autumn afternoon settled its gentle folds around her. He had been driving much too fast.

'Well, that's the end of that,' she muttered into the dying sun, shivering in the wintry-smelling air. She had wanted him out of her life, hadn't she? It was the best thing, wasn't it? Then why did her heart feel so sore and bruised, and why did she have the crazy notion that she had just thrown away something very precious, something she would never be able to replace?

By evening Tania's natural fortitude had asserted itself and she was congratulating herself on escaping intact from a potentially disastrous situation. If her heart gave a little pang when she thought of a certain dark stranger she quelled it immediately, grateful to be back in her own world on her own terms.

She called a friend who worked at the local old folks' home to come and pick up the baskets of flowers, and after she had gone had a long, lazy soak in a hot bath while the last remnants of the heavy perfume dispersed in the evening air

'Banana and jam sandwiches tonight,' she muttered to next door's cat, who visited her periodically, mostly at meal-times. She was sitting curled up in her old fluffy dressing-gown in front of the fire with the cat purring on her lap when the local DJ's strident voice interrupted the 'golden oldies' hour she had been humming along with, causing the plate to fall in a sticky crash from suddenly nerveless fingers.

'We have just been informed that the wealthy Italian businessman who was badly injured in the horrific car crash earlier this afternoon is still fighting for his life in a local hospital tonight. The police are appealing for anyone who saw the accident or was with the injured man this afternoon to come forward. His name is not being released at present until next of kin have been contacted, but if anyone listening has any information which may assist the police with their enquiries it will be treated in strictest confidence. I think that means they are asking for help, folks——'

Tania switched off the facetious voice with hands that trembled, reaching for the telephone directory and dialling the police station as her thoughts raced madly. He couldn't be fighting for his life, he was so vibrant, so alive...

The next few hours were the worst of Tania's life. The police immediately despatched a young constable to get her tearful statement. He was later joined by an older man in plain clothes, who gently explained to her what they knew of the accident.

'It would appear that Mr Meliora lost control of the car on a wet patch in the road,' he said slowly, his world-weary eyes taking in her shocked face. 'Unfortunately there were no witnesses, as far as we know, and we have no idea why he should have tried to swerve at that particular point, as the tyre marks seem to suggest. All we do know for sure is that the accident happened at three-thirty this afternoon, through a local farmer who was in his fields at the time and heard the crash. That would be just after you say he left you, miss?'

She nodded tensely, her face turning white.

'Thank you for your help and your promptness in coming forward. We'll be in touch.' He put a fatherly hand on her shoulder. 'I'd take a couple of aspirin and try to go to sleep—you've had a nasty shock.'

After the two men had gone Tania sat huddled in her chair in frozen misery. This was all her fault! She remembered his furious face as he had driven away, his blazing eyes as they had flicked over her in scornful disdain. She had hurt his pride as well as his face and he hadn't been thinking straight. He was going to die and she would have killed him.

'Please, Lord,' she prayed, falling on her knees suddenly in the small, quiet room, 'please don't let him die. I'll work for him for nothing, I'll work for anybody, do anything, but please, please don't let him die.'

How long she knelt there lost in torment she had no idea afterwards, but eventually she crawled into her cold bed, not bothering to fill her small hot-water bottle as usual, feeling she had no right to be warm and comfortable when a life could be snuffed out at any moment and she was to blame.

Morning brought its own kind of relief. The long black night had seemed endless, and when she had slept briefly for an hour or so her dreams had been so horrific that she had been glad to waken, drenched with cold sweat and shaking, in her own familiar bed.

An idea that had been born in the cold early hours of dawn crystallised in the clear light of day. It would take her an hour or so to walk to Great Oaks if she kept up a steady pace; she would need that time to decide what to say when she got there.

The sunlight that greeted her when she left the house had no warmth, but its hue had a brilliance found only in a fine autumn morning. She decided to approach Great Oaks by skirting the perimeter of the town, preferring the woodland slopes to harsh concrete. She had walked this way just a few weeks before, when rowan and briars had been bright with scarlet berries, the bracken a warm glow on the hillsides, and masses of autumnal syca-mores had set the farms and cottages aflame with its richness.

'I was happy that day,' she muttered bewilderedly into the frosty air. 'How can things have changed so fast?'

It was still quite early when she reached Great Oaks, entering the long, perfectly kept gravelled drive which led to the great stone house with her legs shaking. What if they told her he had died? 'He can't die,' she said defiantly into the huge oak trees lining the drive from which the house got its name, 'I won't let him.'

'*Si?*' The tall dark woman who answered her timid knock had obviously just been crying, and Tania's heart turned over with fear. '*Si?* I can help you?' The woman's cheeks were streaked with tears, but her brown eyes were friendly as she looked into Tania's pale face.

'I've just called to see how Mr Meliora is,' Tania said hesitantly, filled with foreboding. 'I wondered if there is anything I could do to help?'

'You know the *signore* he live here? How you know this?' The brown eyes were suddenly mistrustful, and the woman took a step back into the house as though to close the door.

'It's all right,' Tania said hastily, 'Mr Meliora inter-viewed me for a job yesterday, to help the nanny and do some secretarial work for him.'

Her words seemed to reassure the Italian woman slightly, as she opened the door wide again, her slanted eyes watchful. 'Your name, *signorina*?'

'Tania Miles.'

The woman thought for a moment, and then her expression cleared. 'Ah, yes, Signor Meliora he tell me your name. There were four of you at the *albergo*...the hotel?'

'Probably.' Tania smiled nervously. 'I didn't see the others. I was the last. He offered me the job,' she added hopefully. The woman stared at her blankly. 'That's why I came,' Tania said slowly and clearly, 'to see if I could help.'

'*Scusi, signorina, scusi.*' The woman's hand came out to touch her sleeve welcomingly. 'My English, she is slow. Please to come in.'

The beautiful, gleaming wood-panelled hall was as large as Tania's whole flat, the carpet thick and deep and the stairs in the distance stretching endlessly upwards, but Tania only had eyes for the thin figure in front of her. 'How is Mr Meliora?' she repeated anxiously. 'He's not...?'

'No, no.' The woman's face lit up. 'The news he is good. Signor Meliora is...better. He can have the *conversazione.*'

'Oh, thank goodness.' There was a faint ringing in her ears and a rushing blackness before her eyes. Tania had never fainted in her life, but she had the awful feeling she was about to do so now. 'Please...'

The woman caught her as she staggered, guiding her to a small ornate padded chair to one side of the hall and sitting her down firmly. 'The big breaths, you take the big breaths,' she said anxiously, patting Tania's limp hands ineffectually.

'You must think I'm crazy,' Tania murmured apologetically as the faintness began to recede. 'I come here to help and then practically pass out on you.'

'Pass out?' The deep brown eyes were puzzled, and then the homely face broke into a beaming smile. 'Ah,

sì, whoosh!' She did a passable parody of someone col-
lapsing on the floor. 'You have eaten *colazione*? The
breakfast?' As Tania shook her head she clucked her
disapproval.

'Come and eat. The *bambini*, they eat. I am Gilda.'
She helped Tania up gently. 'The hospital, he say I can
take the *bambini* later. You know the *direzione*?'

'Yes, I know where it is,' said Tania eagerly. 'I'll come
with you if you like.'

'*Sì, sì*, I like.'

The children proved to be small replicas of their
handsome father. Emmanuele was little more than a
baby, his small chubby face already showing signs of the
determination that was written in Enrico's hard features. Louisa, the little girl, was more shy, her long black
hair looped into a high pony-tail and her huge brown
eyes serious and reserved.

'They know little of the accident,' Gilda whispered
warningly in her ear as they sat down to eat at the huge
kitchen table. 'They see him soon.' Tania nodded in
agreement.

The cook and housekeeper seemed very friendly, big,
full-blown women in their late fifties and obviously
sisters. 'I'm Daisy, she's May,' one of them informed
her in a broad Yorkshire accent as she passed her a plate
of eggs and bacon, putting a rack of hot toast in front
of her a few seconds later. The atmosphere was genial
and warm, and for the first time in twelve hours Tania
could feel herself beginning to relax.

The morning sped by as she helped Gilda with the
children. She had been surprised to find they both spoke
excellent English. 'The *signore*, he want it that way,'
Gilda explained as Tania expressed her astonishment.

'They have to teach me,' she smiled ruefully and Tania grinned in sympathy.

'I'll help you if you like,' she offered impulsively, but as she did so a little warning bell sounded in her mind. Once Enrico knew she was here he might well dismiss her instantly—she had no idea how he would react. Perhaps he would be too ill to care? She would have to see. Her stomach jolted suddenly at the thought of facing him again.

By the time they left for the hospital after a delicious lunch Tania was feeling much better. The hard work and good food had cleared her mind and steadied her churning stomach. She hadn't done anything wrong! He had offered her the job, after all, before she had refused it, she thought to herself, sticking out her chin as though going into battle, which was exactly how she felt.

A young white-coated doctor met them outside Enrico's room, along with a brisk middle-aged sister, who looked astounded at seeing the children. 'You can't possibly take them in,' she said sharply to Gilda, who looked at her blankly. 'Mr Meliora is very ill.'

'It's all right, Sister,' the doctor said soothingly. 'We thought a brief visit would put Mr Meliora's mind at rest. Frankly if he's the way he is now when he's ill I dread to think what he's like normally.' The sister swept away in a crackle of disapproval as Tania smiled understandingly at the tired, rueful face in front of her.

'Is he being a difficult patient?' she asked quietly.

'We've had better.' He smiled wryly. 'I can't remember worse.'

'What are his injuries?' asked Tania hesitantly as Gilda looked from one to the other, plainly out of her depth in this foreign country with its incomprehensible language.

'Not as bad as we thought. Concussion was a problem but he's over that now, and we've ascertained that internal injuries are slight—three cracked ribs, which are causing him some discomfort but not enough to keep him in bed. I feel like putting a guard on the door at the moment. The determination of the man is amazing. He doesn't seem to realise what a close shave he's had.'

Tania nodded in total agreement. 'I know just what you mean.'

'He was on the critical list for the first few hours but sheer will-power brought him through. The danger is that he will drive himself too fast too soon, but I really don't see how we can stop him.' The doctor looked at her for suggestions, but Tania stared at him blankly.

'Anyway,' the doctor sighed wearily, 'take the children in for a short visit for now.'

Tania didn't know what she expected to see as they tentatively opened the door but it certainly wasn't the glowering face that met her startled eyes. 'Where the hell are my clothes, Nurse...?' The furious voice died away as the children snatched their hands away from Gilda's grasp and flung themselves at their father, their excited voices jabbering rapidly in quick-fire Italian as they climbed up beside him on the narrow hospital bed. Tania saw the dark face wince as they made contact with his body, but the muscled arms went out to hug them to him in a firm hold as he looked over their heads to where Tania and Gilda stood hesitating in the doorway.

'Come in and shut the damn door,' he said irritably, his dark eyes narrowed with enquiry on Tania's face. 'And to what do I owe the pleasure of your company?' His deep voice was maliciously sarcastic.

'Why do you think I'm here?' she bit back immediately, and the black eyes flicked mockingly over her flushed face.

'Come to hold my hand?'

She flushed a still brighter shade of pink. She had noticed he was stripped to the waist apart from a wad of bandages wrapped round his torso, and the sight of the big brown body was doing bizarre things to her insides. He dominated the small white room with his dark presence, his maleness leaping out at her in stark challenge.

'I thought I could perhaps help Gilda with the children when I heard about the accident,' she said stiffly, trying to keep her eyes fixed on a point just over his head.

'How thoughtful.' His voice was cutting. 'You haven't come to gloat, then?'

'You ungrateful swine!' Her blue eyes shot white-hot splinters into his. 'I was concerned about you, though I can't imagine why! I might have known a little thing like a car accident wouldn't make you into a normal human being.'

'*Scusi, Signor Meliora*?' Gilda's English might not have been very good, but even she had had no difficulty in following the heated exchange and she was clearly wondering if she had done the right thing in letting Tania accompany her.

'*Mi dispiace, Gilda.*' He spoke directly to the woman for some moments in swift Italian, and whatever he said it obviously put her mind at rest, for she flashed a quick nervous smile at him as he finished.

The children had been quite oblivious to their father's rage—they were clearly used to his fiery nature. '*Papà,*' Louisa caught his attention as she knelt up on the bed and placed a small brown hand on his chest, 'this is Tania.'

He looked at his daughter for a long moment and then turned his dark eyes up to Tania again, the expression unreadable. 'It would seem I need to be corrected by my daughter,' he said slowly, a flash of self-mockery turning the black eyes into glittering pools. 'How do you do, Tania? It was so good of you to come.'

She looked at him in consternation, totally at a loss as to how to reply. He smiled lazily, noting her confusion. 'That's the second time I've left you speechless.' The red colour that had just subsided leapt into her face again as he reminded her of their passionate exchange the last time they had met.

'Yes, well...' She saw the black eyes were alive with laughter. 'I really was concerned.'

'I would like to believe that,' he said quietly, holding her troubled eyes firmly as all amusement fled from his.

She swallowed a sudden lump in her throat and wrenched her eyes away from his, glancing down at the children in his arms as she did so. It was a mistake. The sight of them cuddled against the broad strong chest where the dark tiny hairs curled damp against his gleaming skin made her blood pound and her hands suddenly moist.

'Do I take it you have reconsidered my offer?' The drawling voice brought her agitated eyes up to his.

'Yes, if it's still open,' she replied stiffly, trying to sound cool and businesslike. 'I shall quite understand if you'd prefer——'

'What I would prefer is to have you working for me.' He noticed her tenseness. 'It would be a permanent position, Tania, until circumstances changed.' It was the second time he had said her name and her stomach twisted as the lazy deep voice gave it a subtle inflexion, the slight accent adding a seductive charm she was sure her parents had never intended.

'Yes, I understand that.'

'What made you change your mind?' He looked at her full in the face. 'The accident?' She nodded slowly. 'Well, well, it's amazing the things that come out of a seeming disaster.'

Her eyes were bright with remorse, and his own suddenly tightened with intuition. 'You don't think you are to blame in any way for that?' She looked at him bleakly, her face speaking volumes. 'You silly girl.' His voice was more tender than she had heard it before. 'It was totally my own fault. I am too experienced a driver to let anything interfere with my concentration, but I forgot to take into account the wildlife in this part of your country. A fox slipped across the road in front of me and I didn't want to hit it.' He looked slightly shamefaced. 'I didn't.'

'You hit a tree, though.' A shred of humour showed in her face, and he smiled back at her easily.

'The tree survived and so did I. The car is incidental. I consider the story had a happy ending.'

She looked at him, shaking her head slightly. 'You could have been killed.'

'Then that would have been due to my misjudgement.'

He winced again as one of the children moved against him, and Tania moved forward to lift them from the bed, passing them to Gilda as she did so.

'I'm glad you're here. You can go and find what they have done with my clothes.'

'What?' Tania stared at him as he looked up at her, impatience written in every chiselled line of his face.

'For goodness' sake, woman. Gilda is the one who doesn't understand English.' His voice was back to its old scathing note. 'It's perfectly simple: I don't want to walk out of here stark naked. It might upset some of the old ladies.' His eyes gleamed wickedly as he saw the quick colour rise in her cheeks.

'You can't leave yet.' She looked at him, horrified. 'You've been involved in a very serious accident; they won't let——'

'I don't give a damn what they will let. I'm coming home now with or without clothes. I was going to call a taxi, but having the car here is an added advantage.'

'You can't!' As he made to draw back the sheets covering him she moved hastily towards the door. 'Wait a moment—I'll get the doctor.'

An hour later they were speeding home in Gilda's smart little blue runabout. Enrico had insisted on driving and, after the taut scene with the hospital staff and a very dignified consultant, who had become a lot less dignified as the conversation with his patient had progressed, Tania had had no strength left to argue with him.

His clothes had been damaged beyond saving, so he was dressed in a pair of hospital pyjamas and a faded blue dressing-gown, which still managed to look incredibly good on the big bronzed figure at her side. She was horribly conscious that he was in a great deal of pain; the lines round his mouth were stark white, and his tanned face had a grey tinge she didn't like, but he brushed any enquiry aside with a mounting irritation.

'Look.' He pulled up suddenly at the side of the road as in the distance they saw that large predator, a buzzard, soaring effortlessly in the darkening sky. As he cut the engine for a moment, pointing out the huge bird to the children in the back seat, the shrill fluting of a misselthrush hung on the evening air and a shaft of dying sunlight illuminated an old stone farmhouse in the distance. 'This is a beautiful country.' His voice was warm as he looked at her by his side, and his eyes looked into the distance with a depth of sadness in them she could only wonder at. Presently the buzzard was lost against the dark background of the hillside, and with a deep sigh he started the engine as the children complained of growing pangs of hunger.

Later that night, back in her own little flat, the enormity of what she had done washed over Tania in great billowing waves. It had seemed so right at the time, and she had been so relieved to find out his injuries weren't as severe as she had been led to expect that her own natural reticence had been swept aside in a flood of euphoria. How could she have been so stupid?

The unease she had felt when she had first met him returned a hundredfold. He lived in an alien world, a world of fast cars and even faster women. She was like a child walking on the top of a crumbling slippery cliff— one wrong move and she would be hurtled out into space, to land, crushed and broken, on the harsh jagged rocks beneath.

CHAPTER FOUR

THE next day started badly and deteriorated thereafter. Mrs Jenkins woke Tania very early by banging on her door, her thin face grim and cold. 'It's come to my attention, Miss Miles, that you've been seen carrying on with some man in a flashy car right outside this house.'

'What?' Tania rubbed her eyes sleepily, glancing at her watch as she pulled her dressing-gown more tightly round her.

'Do you deny it?'

'I haven't the faintest idea what you are talking about, Mrs Jenkins,' Tania said wearily as she shivered in the early-morning chill. She hadn't got to sleep until after two, and it was only six o'clock now.

'Haven't you, now?' The other woman's face was triumphant. 'Lying won't improve matters. I have it on good authority that you were seen with this man the day before yesterday, when you told me you were going for an interview. Funny sort of interview if you ask me! Is this the man who sent you those flowers?'

'I had a lift home with my employer, Mrs Jenkins.' Tania's face was now as cold as her landlady's. 'I consider our relationship is our own business.'

'Oh, you've got a job now, then?' The narrow face looked crestfallen for a brief moment. 'Well, it doesn't make any difference to what I want to say. I want you out, Miss Miles, out of my house by the end of the week. I've no idea what your ''job'' entails, but if it's what I think it is you ought to be careful. You'll be had up by the police, you will.'

'I beg your pardon?' Tania took a step forward, her face livid, as the older woman backed away nervously. She realised too late that she had gone too far this time. 'Let me tell you something, Mrs Jenkins, something I've been wanting to say to you for a long, long time: you are a nasty, spiteful, shrivelled-up old crone without a decent thought in your head. Only you could come up with an insulting supposition like that and then have the nerve to accuse me of it without a shred of evidence. I have no intention of justifying myself to you, and, as for your precious flat, you can keep it! I'll move out when I've got somewhere else to go, and you can wait until then.'

'I will not!' The other woman backed to the top of the narrow stairs, putting a few feet between her and the tigress she had aroused. 'You owe three months' rent and I'm evicting you herewith. You try and stay and I'll cause such a stink that you won't get anywhere else in this town. My nephew has moved down here to go to college and I need the flat. I want you out by Saturday.'

'That's ridiculous.' Tania tried to speak calmly. 'Today is Tuesday—I'm never going to find anywhere at such short notice.'

'Perhaps your boyfriend can put you up—he seems keen enough. If not, then you can sleep on the streets for all I care.'

'You can't do that.' Tania looked at the bony vindictive face without moving. 'Legally you haven't got a leg to stand on.'

'We'll see about that.' The voice was malicious. 'At any rate, you'll rue the day you crossed me. I can make things very difficult for you, my girl, if I tell a few of the right people about all your goings-on.'

'There have been no "goings-on", as you so charmingly put it, except in your imagination. Good day, Mrs Jenkins.' Tania shut the door firmly, cutting off any further conversation, and stood for a moment with her back resting against it, her legs trembling. What a vicious old cat! She breathed deeply, fighting back the tears. She had never liked the older woman in the three years she had lived here, but the flat had been so convenient for the children's home just a few streets away, and the Browns' home had been even closer. It had been so thrilling to have her own place too, after the poky room she had rented for a few months when she had first moved down here away from her parents' home. Still, it was clearly time to go—but where? Great Oaks jumped immediately into her mind, but she pushed the thought away hurriedly. She couldn't live in the same house as Enrico, she just couldn't.

She was no nearer a solution when she arrived, breathless and late, at Great Oaks later that morning. She had called in the estate agent's on her way to work but it had been a fruitless exercise, as had her enquiries at the local paper shop. 'There's nowhere that I know of,' the elderly newsagent had said, shaking his grey head slowly. 'Hasn't been for months, love.'

'You have decided to grace us with your presence, then?' The cold, barbed voice froze her as she walked tentatively down the hall after opening the door of Great Oaks with the key Gilda had given her last night.

'Good morning.' She turned as she spoke, to see Enrico standing in the doorway of the room he was using as his study. He was dressed and shaven but clearly in a great deal of pain. The big body was hunched over slightly and his face had a grey tinge reminiscent of the previous day. 'You don't look too good.'

'That's just what I wanted to hear.' The deep voice held a note of mocking exasperation. 'You are obviously going to be a ray of sunshine to have around the place.'

'You didn't employ me to be a ray of sunshine,' she bit back sharply, her face flushing at the scorn in his voice.

'I did employ you to be here on time, though.' His eyes were cool and there was a ferocious scowl on his face. 'I expect punctuality at all times, and I've already been waiting for you for nearly an hour.'

'I'm sorry.' She forced the words through stiff lips. 'There was a good reason I was late this morning and I'll make sure it doesn't happen again. I didn't realise the hours were so rigid. I expected to stay later tonight to make up the time.'

He looked at her for a long moment and then ran his hand over his face as he moved carefully back into his study. 'Come in here a minute.'

She followed him into the room warily. What now? She couldn't take much more this morning. He walked slowly across to the desk in the far corner and lowered himself into the big leather chair cautiously, but even so beads of sweat broke out on his brow and his lips were white with pain.

'You should be in bed.' She spoke out of real concern, but he waved his hand irritably, keeping his head lowered until some colour crept back into his face.

'Bed is useful for sleeping and a certain other pastime I won't mention,' he said caustically as he raised his eyes to hers. 'I have no intention of lying up there like a beached whale. I have work to do and I need to get on with it.' He paused. 'However, before we begin I would

mention that you were right in your assumption that the
hours are flexible. I apologise for my sharpness this
morning. I thought you had changed your mind.'

'That's all right.' Tania's voice was warm with understanding. 'I don't suppose you slept much last night?'

'That has nothing to do with it.' His voice was distant.
'I spoke out of turn and I ask your forgiveness. It is not
a good way to start our working relationship.'

He obviously allowed himself no weakness, Tania
thought ruefully as she looked into the proud face
watching her closely. It must be galling for him to feel
so helpless at the moment.

She smiled cheerfully. 'Apology accepted. Shall we
start work?'

By the end of the morning she was mentally and phys-
ically exhausted, and utterly amazed at the astute and
razor-sharp mind that ate up the work so avidly. If he
was like this when he could barely move with the pain
that kept turning his face white, how could she survive
when he was better?

'Mr Meliora?' she asked as he paused for breath in
the middle of dictating a long and complicated report.
'Could we stop for a while?'

He looked at her as she sat, stiff and cramped in the
seat opposite him, flexing the muscles in her hand that
were aching intolerably. 'What's the time?' He looked
at the gold watch on his wrist and his eyes narrowed in
surprise. 'Good grief, girl, why didn't you stop me
before? You must be starving. Come on.'

He rose with obvious difficulty, brushing her offer of
help away with a black frown. 'You've been a great help
this morning, Tania.' He steadied himself for a fraction
of a second on the polished surface of the big desk.

'There's just one thing that was wrong.' She looked at him enquiringly. 'The name is Enrico.'

'Oh, but I couldn't; Gilda calls you——'

'I know what Gilda calls me.' His voice was curt. 'And you will use my first name. It isn't a request.' She looked at him uncertainly and his expression softened fractionally. 'Gilda's family has been in our employ for many, many years. It would be unthinkable to her to use my Christian name, although I have suggested it in the past; her parents are steeped in the old ways and have brought her up accordingly. However, you are a modern miss,' the intonation was mocking, 'and it would be just as unnatural for us to indulge in meaningless formality.'

'I don't think——'

'Tania!' Her name was a bark. 'I don't want another battle of wills over this. For goodness' sake, girl, accept what I say and leave it alone.' He muttered something that sounded acutely rude in Italian as he opened the door for her to leave, his face unsmiling. 'I have never met an English girl who is so argumentative. Are you like this with everyone?'

She shook her head crossly. 'No, I'm not. I can get on with anyone, as it happens.' A brief picture of Mrs Jenkins flashed into her mind, but she resolutely ignored it.

'I'll have to take your word for that in the circumstances. You'd certainly make a great Italian grandmother—that's all I can say.'

'Why?' she asked curiously as they walked together along the wide hall towards the kitchen.

'They rule their families with a rod of iron.' She didn't think, somehow, it was meant as a compliment.

'I'm sorry I don't come up to your expectations,' she said stiffly, feeling ridiculously hurt.

He glanced at her out of the corner of his eye, his face rueful. 'Believe me, Tania, if I had had any expectations you more than fulfil them.' He put his finger to her lips as she went to reply. 'Now please shut up and let's find something to eat in this establishment.'

'Oh, there you are, sir.' Daisy's cheerful voice greeted them as he opened the kitchen door, her round red face comically like that of her sister's, who was busy at the stove. 'I was just coming along to tell you lunch will be ready in ten minutes, if that's all right? I've already set the places in the dining-room.'

'That's very good of you, Daisy,' Enrico said gravely. 'We'll just have time for a sherry, then. Where are Gilda and the children?'

'They'll be back any minute, sir. Just gone for a little walk to put some roses in the bairns' cheeks. They had an early lunch and Gilda wanted them to have some fresh air before their afternoon nap.'

He nodded and shut the door as May almost dropped a large pie-dish she was carrying to the kitchen table, her plump face scarlet and flustered. It was clear they both found the master of the house somewhat intimidating. Tania could sympathise with them wholeheartedly.

'Come.' He took her arm lightly and led her along the hall, opening a door at the far end. 'You would like a sherry? Or maybe you would prefer a glass of wine?'

She was still standing, transfixed, in the doorway as he spoke—the magnificent room had quite taken her breath away.

'It's beautiful.' The words were a soft sigh but enough to catch his attention as he opened the drinks cabinet in a small alcove.

'What?' He turned questioningly, his dark brows raised in enquiry. 'Oh, the room; yes, it is very pleasant.' She looked at him quickly to see if he was being deliberately offhand, but the cool, arrogant face was genuinely uninterested. It was just another indication of the different worlds in which they moved, she thought miserably to herself. The room was exquisitely furnished with dark wood antiques, scattered high-backed chairs and settees in grey buttoned velvet, complemented perfectly by the pale pink thick-piled carpet and dusky pink and grey curtains hanging to one side of the full-length windows, which overlooked the stately gardens at the rear of the house. The noble high ceiling was beautifully engraved and the regal old fireplace had a roaring log fire crackling in its depths, giving a feeling of warmth and welcome in all the grandeur.

'Have you thought any more about moving in here?' he asked as he handed her a glass of pale cream sherry, gesturing for her to be seated. She moved slowly to one of the chairs and sat gingerly on the edge, taking a sip of the drink before she replied, her mind racing.

'Not really,' she lied hesitantly. 'I've always lived away from my work.'

'It would be more convenient for all concerned if you were on hand,' he answered smoothly, his dark eyes gleaming as he stood with his back to the fire, his face tight and watchful. 'You are, of course, free to use one of the cars whenever you wish. You can drive, I take it?'

'Yes, my parents paid for lessons for my eighteenth birthday,' she answered automatically, another part of her brain wondering if she should tell him about the conversation with Mrs Jenkins and her imminent homelessness. For some reason she couldn't fathom she shrank

from revealing her problem to this giant of a man who
seemed to sweep aside all obstacles in his own way and
that of everyone around him. He would expect her to
come and live at Great Oaks, and she felt chilled and
frightened at the thought of being so close to his orbit,
so completely in his power. With her flat there was still
a little independence left, a bolt-hole! She felt a sudden
shock as the thought occurred to her, but realised it was
true; she needed a bolt-hole.

'Now why are those big blue eyes so far away?' he
asked softly, causing her head to snap up and meet his
intent gaze. 'Why do I always get the feeling that if I
could read your thoughts I wouldn't like what they said?'

It was so near the truth that she couldn't stop the
burning flush flooding her face with guilty colour.

'Hmm.' The deep voice was cold. 'I seem to have hit
a nerve.'

She was saved from replying by the arrival of the
children, who crashed open the door and scampered into
the room in a rush of cold air and red noses. '*Papà*!'
Louisa shouted exuberantly, followed by a stream of
Italian, leaping up into the strong arms like a small
monkey. Tania saw Enrico wince as the little girl landed
against his body, and he moved slowly to one of the big
settees, setting her down carefully to one side of him and
drawing Emmanuele up into the circle of his other arm.

'Talk English, Louisa,' he said gently to his small
daughter as he kissed the top of her dark head gently.
'Tania doesn't understand our language, and it is not
polite to leave her out of our conversation, is it?'

'Sorry, Tania.' The small girl was quite unabashed.
'Are you going to stay with us for a little while?'

'Yes, if you'll have me,' Tania replied, smiling at the
friendly little face lifted up to hers.

'Then I will teach you Italian,' Louisa said determinedly. 'Would you like that?'

'Very much,' Tania replied gently, conscious of Enrico's mocking eyes sweeping her face, 'but I'm here to work really, Louisa.'

'You'll have plenty of time with the children,' Enrico said silkily, his voice soft. 'It is a very good suggestion. If you accompany us to Italy for several months of the year it will be necessary for you to learn some of the basic vocabulary.'

'I'm going to be very busy, *Papà*,' Louisa said importantly, looking up into her father's laughing face as she spoke. 'I've got to teach Tania Italian, and poor Gilda is not doing very well at English at all. She makes me very cross sometimes because she forgets so quickly.'

'That's enough of that, you precocious infant,' Enrico said with a dry chuckle and a rueful glance in Tania's direction. 'Time for your nap.'

As though on cue, Gilda appeared in the doorway, holding out her hands to the two children, who obediently climbed down from their father's arms and walked towards her. Emmanuele stopped by Tania's chair and looked up at her solemnly, his big brown eyes anxious, one chubby hand resting on her arm. 'Me want you to stay, Nana,' he lisped seriously, his baby voice stumbling over her name. 'Me like you.'

'Thank you, Emmanuele,' she said gravely, her eyes warm on the small flushed face. 'I like you too.'

'Do you like me?' Louisa asked immediately, not wishing to be left out of the compliments. Tania nodded earnestly, and the small girl smiled complacently, clearly satisfied. 'And *Papà?*'

'That's enough, Louisa; off you go.' Enrico's dry voice cut swiftly into the conversation, and as the door closed behind them he turned to Tania with a small smile twisting his mouth. 'What about *Papà*, then?'

She stared at him wordlessly. The glass of sherry on an empty stomach had made her feel slightly light-headed, and speech had quite deserted her. He shook his head slowly, his black eyes holding her nervous blue ones in a tight hold. 'Do you still hate me?' The words were soft and low, his voice compelling, and she felt his sensual magic slide over her flesh in a shivering tide. 'Do you, Tania?'

She shook her head slowly, her thick chestnut hair turned red and gold by the fire's brilliance. 'No, that was a stupid thing to say. I don't hate anyone.'

'I'm not anyone.' A flash of dark arrogance crossed his face, but he controlled his annoyance swiftly as she blinked away her nervousness. 'Your hair is really quite lovely.' He moved across to where she sat and raised her gently by her arms, standing her in front of him and lifting the silky strands in his hands as he looked down into her upturned face. She couldn't have moved to save her life; his dominance was absolute.

'We'd better go through to lunch,' she murmured faintly as she stood still within the circle of his arms, as though hypnotised by the deep, enigmatic power his gentleness was revealing.

'Not until you have answered my question properly.' His voice was a little cruel as he let her hair fall about her shoulders in tumbled disarray. 'I am entitled to know if you have changed your opinion of me in any way.' The flickering firelight caught the silver scar on his cheek, making his bronzed skin darker, and suddenly he seemed menacing and fascinatingly dangerous, like a superb and beautiful black panther that could be docile and slumbrous one moment and then without warning leap for the death-blow.

'I don't know what you want me to say...' Her voice trailed away as he leant over her slightly, a small flame burning in the depths of his eyes.

'Neither do I.' His voice was a whisper as he trailed his lips over her tremulous mouth, his hands clasped behind his back. 'Neither do I, my little English hedgehog.' His accent and the low, almost tender tone of his voice caused her to shudder as he straightened slowly, his eyes curiously rueful.

'Lunch.' Before she could grasp what he had said he had moved her firmly towards the door, his face once again the cold and slightly austere mask she was used to, and as she followed him into the dining-room on legs that shook she felt again that irrational and over-whelming fear that made her want to leave the room and Great Oaks and run, run for her life and hide from this cool, powerful man who could turn her world upside-down with a glance from his glittering eyes.

It was late evening when she left Great Oaks, and then in circumstances she could not have imagined. She worked all afternoon in the study, clearing most of the mountain of paperwork Enrico had dictated earlier, while the blue-grey sky outside the window slowly turned into dark slate as dusk encroached upon the garden. Gilda and the children joined her for a tea-time snack about four, and Gilda told her Enrico expected her to stay for dinner, after which he had said he would run her home personally.

'He's resting upstairs,' Gilda explained slowly. 'He is *malato*—how you say, ill?'

'He is pushing himself too hard,' Tania said with a worried frown. 'He only came out of hospital yesterday, for goodness' sake. Is he always like this?'

'*Sì*.' Gilda nodded despondently. 'Ever since their *madre*—their mother—died.' She cast a glance at the children, who were sitting in rapt silence in front of the television set, watching a particularly violent and bloodthirsty cartoon. 'Now it is all work.'

'He must have loved her an awful lot.' Tania's heart had jumped in her chest at the Italian woman's words, although she couldn't have explained why.

Gilda shrugged and her brown eyes slid away from Tania. '*Sì*.' She clearly did not wish to pursue the conversation, and Tania was left with the niggling feeling that there was something she had missed, although the opportunity to ask more was lost when Emmanuele spilt his milk all over himself and his sister.

Just before six she joined Daisy and May in the kitchen for a cup of coffee while Gilda bathed the children ready for bed. Her head was thudding with the amount of typing she had worked through, and she stretched her cramped limbs with a small sigh as she sipped her drink.

'You look done in, love.' As usual Daisy was the spokeswoman, while her sister nodded in the background. 'I should have an early night, if I were you.'

'I will.' Tania nodded wearily. 'I didn't get much sleep last night, and then my landlady woke me at six.'

'You live with that Mrs Jenkins, don't you?' Daisy's eyes were curious. 'Nasty bit of work she is—don't know how you stand her.'

'Neither do I,' Tania said with great feeling, 'but I shan't have to much longer anyway. She's told me I've got to move out at the end of this week.'

'Why is that, then?'

Intent on their conversation, none of the women noticed a tall dark figure standing silently in the open doorway.

'She wants to move her nephew in. I owe three months' rent, although I've told her I'll pay it now I'm working again, but she's decided I'm a bad influence to have around the place, I think. She's great for putting two and two together and making five, but——'

'Could I have a word, Miss Miles?' As the three women swung round Enrico's cool, silky voice sent shivers running down Tania's spine. In spite of his calm voice, she could sense he was furiously angry; his eyes were as hot as lightning as they pierced her face. 'In my study, please.'

He turned and strode down the passageway, not waiting to see if she would follow, confident that his authority would not be flouted. She trailed after him with a sinking heart; why hadn't she told him this morning when she'd had the chance? It was too late now and, with his quick intuition, he would guess exactly why she had kept it from him.

When they were in the study and he had shut the door he stood with his back to her, looking out of the window into the shadowed garden for some time. The old grandfather clock in the corner ticked away the seconds until Tania was on the point of screaming, and she almost did just that as he swung round suddenly, his face black with anger.

'Well?' His voice was a growl. 'Why did you inform my housekeepers of your situation before you told me? You surely realised I would find out sooner or later?'

'Yes! No! I don't know...' She stammered to a halt as she met the full force of his wrath.

'How dare you treat me as though I were stupid? What do you think I am? Some perverted madman who once he gets you into his house will never let you go again? Don't credit yourself so highly, Miss Miles. You have absolutely nothing I want!' His words were vitriolic, but they were nothing to the cold venom that was twisting his face into something unrecognisable. 'As you seem so loath to accept my hospitality, I really think the best thing for all concerned is for you to leave this house and not return.'

She stood, numbed and still, before him, her blue eyes open as wide as they could go and her mouth white with fear.

'Do you hear me? I said get out and stay out!' As he spat out the last words the accumulation of months of worry, added to the shock of her accident and the mind-wrenching horror of his, plus the distasteful scene with Mrs Jenkins that morning, suddenly erupted from her body in a deep well of wailing agony that flooded from her in a torrent of gasping weeping. If the world had exploded into a million pieces she couldn't have felt more wretched than she did in that moment. She tried to move to the door but was blinded and deafened by her own tears, and as she felt his arms reach out and hold her she suddenly collapsed against him, not caring that he was the instigator of all her misery, just needing the warmth of human contact in her anguish.

'*Mi dispiace, mia piccola.*' He was murmuring into her shining hair as he half carried her over to the chair, sitting down and taking her on to his lap in much the same way she had seen him do to the children.

He sat, quietly stroking her hair and murmuring comfortingly in his native tongue until her sobs subsided into soft hiccups. Her face was hidden against his chest, and as the storm of weeping passed she began to feel incredibly embarrassed and horribly aware of the ridiculous spectacle she had made of herself.

'I'm sorry.' She struggled to move away from the hard body enfolding hers, but he thrust a crisp white handkerchief under her nose while his other arm kept a firm grip on her waist.

'Mop up.' His voice was tender with a slight throb of amusement in its depths, and when she raised her swimming eyes to his she surprised a flash of emotion in his face that was gone in an instant as he met her glance. He settled her more comfortably on his lap and sighed with mock disapproval. 'Whatever am I going to do with you? You are a constant surprise. Just when I think I've got you all taped you do something quite extraordinary. How long have you been holding all that in?'

She shrugged awkwardly. He seemed quite unaffected by her closeness, but the smell and feel of his hard body was turning her insides into melted butter.

'Come on. I want some answers.' The teasing note was still in his voice but his expression had set into the steel determination she knew so well.

'It's just been a difficult few months.' She tried to make her voice light but a slight wobble betrayed that tears were still close to the surface.

'Why won't you let me help you? Do you dislike me so much?'

'No, it's not that.' She shook her head slightly, uncomfortably aware of her tear-stained face and tangled hair. She must look such a mess.

'What, then?' He clearly wasn't going to stop until she had told him everything, so, beginning right back

with Melanie at the children's home, she chronicled her
tale of woe beneath his quiet gaze.

'It's just all been so difficult.' His face had hardened
into pure granite when she had repeated her conversation with Mrs Jenkins, and at her last words he gently
moved her off his lap and slowly stood up, walking over
to the door unhurriedly.

'I can understand that. Get your coat, Tania. Mrs
Jenkins we will deal with together and, whether you like
it or not, you are staying here from tonight.' She followed meekly in his wake and stood waiting while he
explained to a surprised Daisy and May that dinner
would be delayed for an hour. 'Could you get a room
organised for Tania too, Daisy? She's going to be living
with us for the foreseeable future. The one next to Gilda
will do nicely—it has its own *en suite*.'

Within minutes they were speeding through the silent,
tranquil countryside, Enrico concentrating on the shadowed road in front of him, his face cool and aloof and
his brown hands relaxed on the steering-wheel. Tania
was anything but relaxed. She was dreading the confrontation ahead. Mrs Jenkins could be maliciously
spiteful in the normal way of things, but when she was
crossed she turned into pure poison.

They reached the big house, still without speaking,
and as she made to get out of the car Enrico put his
hand over hers. 'No. You stay here. It is a furnished
flat?' Tania nodded. 'Then you tell me what to bring
for tonight and we will have the rest of your belongings
sent to Great Oaks in the morning. I do not want you
to see that woman again.'

Tania looked at his grim face nervously. 'What are
you going to say?'

'Something that from the sound of it should have been said a long time ago. It is out of your hands now. You just stay here and I'll return shortly.' He levered himself out of the low seat with obvious difficulty, and she heard his breath catch sharply in his throat as he stood up.

'Please, Enrico. Let me come. You're in no fit state——'

'Be silent.' He looked at her with shuttered eyes. 'This must be done and then you can forget it.' He walked round the side of the car and tapped on her window. 'Her keys?' As she gave them to him a small smile touched the edge of his hard mouth. 'It has taken something of a calamity for you to speak my name, but never mind, it was worth it. It wasn't so hard, was it?' She stared at him in the darkness and he gave a dry chuckle at the expression on her face, his teeth gleaming white in his dark face. 'Don't worry. I won't look on it as a proposal of marriage.'

He was gone before she could reply, and, as she watched him walk purposefully up the steps and disappear into the house, in her heart flowered something that caused her eyes to widen in horror and her face turn pale in the concealing shadows. She loved him. No, it was impossible; not this hard, cold man who had such contempt for women who desired him, suspecting only greed and self-gain in their protestations of love. He had made it clear that the only reason he had offered her the job in the first place was because he could rely on her dislike keeping a firm wedge between them.

She was imagining it! Her mind raced, seeking an escape, but her heart told her the truth. If he were penniless and destitute she would still love him; without knowing it she had loved him from that very first moment when she had looked into his dark face. What

was she to do? She groaned as she rubbed her hand over
her eyes. How could she work with him every day, live
in the same house and eat at the same table and not
betray herself to his observant gaze? She looked down
the months ahead of her with a chill of dread trickling
down her spine, then her back straightened and her small
jaw jutted out in determination. She would do it. She
would never, ever let him suspect her true feelings for
him; she would die first. She wouldn't be just another
lovesick female that he would arrange to dispose of at
the first opportunity, as he had done so many times in
the past. Whatever it cost her, she would walk away from
this with her head held high and her pride intact, even
if it left her heart in ribbons.

CHAPTER FIVE

THE next few weeks settled into a harmonious pattern, and Tania found her transition in to the Meliora household far easier than she had imagined. Her state of mind was helped considerably by the fact that after the first week Enrico was rarely at home. The business deal he was involved with had developed various hiccups, which he didn't trust anyone else to deal with. Consequently he spent much of his time in London, returning briefly at the weekends to see the children and get some rest.

Since that evening in his study he had maintained a friendly, but distant, manner towards her which in the circumstances suited Tania admirably. It gave her time to build up her barrier towards him and she became amazingly adept at concealing her true feelings whenever he was near.

Her relationship with Gilda and the children blossomed swiftly. Apart from two or three mornings a week, when she worked quietly in the study, typing reams from the dictation Enrico left on tape each weekend, she spent all her time with them, and Gilda readily accepted her as one of the family. It was during one of their friendly chats when the children were having their afternoon nap that she learnt more about the autocratic, cold master of Great Oaks.

'How old was Enrico's wife when she died?' Tania asked curiously after Gilda had commented how like her mother little Louisa was.

'She was just twenty-nine,' Gilda replied sadly. 'So *bella*—how you say, beautiful?' Tania nodded, her eyes clouding. 'She had waited for the *signore* for so long, and then to only have *quattro*,' she counted four on her fingers, 'years with him as his wife. So tragic.' She shook her head mournfully.

'Enrico must have been devastated.' Tania felt a small sharp knife twist in her ribs.

'*Sì*.' Gilda looked at her with her big brown spaniel eyes. 'She died giving him a son. It broke his heart.'

'Couldn't anything have been done?' Tania knew she probably shouldn't continue the conversation, but the temptation to find out more about Enrico's past life with the woman he had married was irresistible, even though it was tearing her heart apart.

'My *madre* was in the room with them when the *signora* died. There was too much bleeding when Emmanuele he was born. My mother—she try to help but it is no good. It all happen too fast. The *signore*, he go like crazy man but the *signora*, she is peaceful and calm. She thank him for marrying her and making her so happy and he kisses her and then she die.' Gilda shrugged dismissively. 'My *madre* say it the only time she ever see Signor Meliora cry since he was a tiny *bambino*.'

'That's terrible, Gilda.' Tania's eyes were wide with shock. 'Poor Enrico, and his poor wife. They had known each other a long time?'

'*Sì*.' Gilda nodded. 'Their families are friends from when Enrico and Catalina are *bambini*, and there was great rejoicing when they got married. It is good to join the two estates together, make them *robusti*?'

'Strong, yes,' said Tania in a slightly dazed voice. She was beginning to wish she had never pursued the conversation.

'And they are so happy together, and the *signora* she love him so much. She was very beautiful. It very sad.' Gilda wiped a tear away with the corner of her handkerchief. 'We all cry and the *signore* he lock himself away for days.'

Sudden shrieks from the direction of the nursery brought their talk to an end, but Tania went over the conversation time and time again in the days that followed. How would such an unexpected tragedy have affected Enrico? There was no telling which way that mind would have taken, he was such a mystery—fiery and passionate one minute, cold and aloof the next. Would he have sought comfort from someone or something, or would he have gone further into himself, drawing on his own strength alone and becoming harder because of it?

She looked at him with new eyes the next time she saw him when he arrived home, irritable and tired, for the weekend. Her love for him had made her supersensitive to his every gesture and expression, but, even so, she jolted with a start of surprise on the Saturday morning when she was helping him sort some papers in the study.

'Have I grown two heads in the last week, Tania?' The deep velvet voice was dry with puzzled humour.

'Sorry?' She looked at him warily from beneath her long lashes.

'It's just that every time I catch you looking at me there's a strange look on your face. I know something is being hatched in that busy little brain of yours, but I can't put my finger on it at the moment.'

Thank goodness for that, Tania breathed silently. She forced a casual light smile to her face. 'I haven't a clue what you are talking about, Enrico,' she lied pleasantly. 'Perhaps you've been working too hard?'

'Now that's a definite possibility,' he agreed sombrely, his dark eyes flicking to his briefcase, which was bulging with tapes and papers. 'However, part of the last few weeks' workload has been to ensure we can get away to Italy in time for Christmas. I'd like to leave the week before, if that is convenient for you?'

'Yes, that's fine,' Tania answered quickly. 'I'll let my parents know today.'

'I would like to talk to them when you ring.' It was an order.

'Why?' She looked at him in surprise.

'Your father will need to be satisfied that his daughter is in good hands.' He sounded all Italian. 'It is necessary for me to set their minds at rest.'

'But it's not like that in England,' she protested slowly. 'I'm twenty-four years old, Enrico, and——'

He interrupted her abruptly, his dark face autocratic. 'It is like that everywhere, Tania. I am a father. I have a father's heart.'

'But——'

'Tania, please.' He shut his eyes briefly, as he was apt to do when finding her trying. 'I can work hard all day but it doesn't compare with the exhaustion I feel after a few minutes' battling with you. Now close that delectable mouth and lower those beautiful blue eyes and try and pretend for once that you are a nice, submissive Italian girl.'

She glanced at his dark sensual face—there had been laughter in his voice. 'I thought Italian women were very volatile.'

'Believe me, my little English hedgehog, they can't begin to compare with you.'

'I wish you wouldn't call me a hedgehog. It isn't very flattering.' Her voice was childishly defiant.

He looked at her intently and she glanced away quickly; those brilliant dark eyes could read her mind. 'On the contrary.' His voice held no laughter now. 'Have you ever looked closely at one?'

'I can't say I've made a study of them, no.' She tried to lighten the strangely intimate mood that had sprung up unnoticed between them as her heart began to flutter madly and her hands grew suddenly damp.

'They have the most exquisite little faces.' The dark voice ran over her nerves like soft cream. 'And, although their bodies have sharp spikes on the outside, the inside is wonderfully soft and warm. Far better than the other way round, don't you think?'

She looked at him without speaking, her blue eyes caught by the banked fire in his.

'Far too many women of my acquaintance keep their barbs safely hidden until they think they are in control.' A flash of bitterness blazed across his features as he touched the scar on his face abruptly, his expression softening as his eyes returned to her puzzled frown. 'You have no idea what I mean, do you?'

She shook her head slowly.

'Good; keep it that way. Let's just say a memento from a jealous woman is not always what you expect.'

She stood quite still as he moved towards her, lifting her chin up so her eyes were forced to meet his. 'Now are you going to let me speak to your parents?' She nodded silently. 'That's a good girl.' He dropped what was obviously intended as a casual kiss on her half-open mouth, but as his warm lips met hers a spark seemed to ignite between them, and with a muttered exclamation he pulled her to him, his breathing suddenly harsh.

'Tania.' He groaned her name against her skin, his mouth suddenly devouring hers in a long, deep kiss that had her moving into his body, pressing closer to the hard frame that held her so tightly. With a shuddering sigh his hands moved down to her hips, holding her against his iron limbs while his mouth drank from hers like a thirsty man sating his dryness.

A wild kind of exhilaration filled her as she felt him trembling against her, all fear swept away as she savoured the feel of being in his arms. Her arms slid up round his taut, strong neck, and as they did so he nearly lifted her off her feet with his passion, his hands running over her body in an agony of desire.

'Stop this. Move away.' His voice was a plea but one she was incapable of answering. She had dreamed of being in his embrace so often over the last few weeks, but the reality was breathtaking. She clung to him as he bent over her, his experienced hands invoking whimpers of pleasure as he covered her face in small hungry kisses, his mouth warm against her eyelids, throat, hair, his hands urgent on her bare skin.

'No! Tania!' He thrust her away from him so sharply that she would have fallen but for his hand reaching out immediately to steady her. He turned and leant with both hands on the desk, his big body hunched and his breathing hard and laboured.

'Enrico?' The sound of her small lost voice seemed to bring him back to himself, and he took a deep shuddering breath as he turned to face her again, his face tight and stiff.

'I'm sorry, Tania.' His voice had a huskiness he couldn't control. 'I didn't mean that to happen.'

She stared at him, frightened to make any move that would cause him to reject her further, her eyes huge and blank in her white face.

'Don't look like that; it's all right.' He made to put his hand on her shoulder but stopped himself. 'You haven't known a man before, have you?' She knew what he meant and her face flushed with hot humiliation. Had her inexperience been so painfully obvious? She lowered her eyes as she shook her head, her glowing red-brown hair fanning her face in silky feathers.

'A few more seconds and I would have been unable to stop. Do you understand me?' His voice was gruff. She nodded as the realisation dawned that she hadn't wanted him to stop. If he had taken her, right there on the carpet, she wouldn't have been able to resist. In fact, she had actively encouraged him, she thought with burning shame as she remembered her uninhibited response to his lovemaking. How could she have behaved so wantonly, knowing he didn't care for her at all?

'The first time should be special, with someone you love and with someone who loves you. It shouldn't be thrown away in a moment's passion.' His voice was gentle but she heard it through a dark haze. Was that what he thought of her? That she had responded to him like that with just animal desire? 'It was wrong of me to use my experience to seduce you, but please believe me, it wasn't intentional.' Everything he said was making the pain worse; she took a deep breath and looked up, her face white.

'I understand, Enrico. Can I go now?'

He looked at her for a long moment and then nodded quietly, his dark face unreadable. 'Of course. I'll see you at dinner, and please, Tania...' she turned at the door and looked at him blankly. '...forget this ever happened.'

As she shut the door and walked over to the stairs to go to her room she felt a tide of feeling rise in her that she could not have described to anyone. A wild rage of love and hate mixed together that brought her to her knees by her bed in an agony of silent weeping. She remembered his hands on her body, the intimate caresses, and something in her shrivelled and died at the thought that he believed she would respond like that to any man. How could he think that? At the same time a little voice in her head reminded her with desperate honesty that she had given him no reason to think otherwise.

At last, tired and spent, she curled into a tight little ball on her bed and shut her eyes miserably, wishing with all her heart that she had not strayed into the orbit of this brilliant black star that was threatening to smash her into a hundred tiny pieces.

She must have dozed off to sleep, because a light knock woke her some time later and she was surprised to see the room was filled with soft mauve shadows, the night sky black with a myriad tiny twinkling stars outside the big picture window directly opposite her bed. 'Come in.' Her voice was a little cracked, and she sat up hastily, smoothing her hair into some sort of order as the door opened.

'Nana!' Emmanuele's baby voice shouted her name and he hurled himself over to the bed, clambering up as Gilda and Louisa followed him into the room. 'Me wanted to play wiv you an you weren't there.' His voice was reproachful.

'The *signore* tell us your head bad.' Gilda's eyes were sympathetic. 'It OK now?'

He thought of everything! Tania nodded. 'Much better, thanks. What's the time?'

'Time for the children's bath.' The deep cold voice from the doorway made them all jump. 'Emmanuele was quite determined he couldn't face the water without you.' Enrico's dark eyes flashed over her red-rimmed eyes and tangled hair before he turned and left. 'We'll see you in a moment in their bathroom for the ceremonial washing.'

Gilda hastily caught the children's hands as she followed Enrico from the room, but Emmanuele put up such loud and deafening resistance against leaving Tania that she put a hand on the Italian woman's arm understandingly. 'I'll bring him along in a minute, Gilda, when I've washed my face.'

Gilda nodded gratefully. She adored the children, but Emmanuele's rages were quite beyond her ability to deal with.

He sat on the bed, jabbering away in his pidgin English as she washed, adorably docile now he had got his own way. She glanced at him out of the corner of her eye as she brushed her hair into a sleek high pony-tail, and he caught the look and grinned disarmingly, quite aware he had won yet another battle with his Italian nanny. 'Gidda gone,' he said solemnly.

'You're really a little rascal,' said Tania smilingly as she sat down beside him for a moment on the bed. He climbed immediately into her arms, his chubby body pressed close to hers.

'Me not want Gidda,' he said as he wrapped his arms round her neck and planted a big wet kiss on her cheek. 'Me want you.' She hugged him close as she reflected ruefully that he had all his father's elusive charm as well as quite a bit of his own.

She had got to know the children quite well in the last few weeks and had found they were as different as chalk and cheese. Louisa was a bright, sunny little girl who loved everyone and everything without reservation, easy to handle and a joy to be with. Emmanuele, on the other hand, was a turbulent mixture of fire and bewitching meekness, with surprisingly definite likes and dislikes for one so young. He adored his father, loved Louisa with offhand brotherly affection, and tolerated Gilda with indulgent childish cruelty, often reducing the Italian woman to tears at his refusal to obey her.

His devotion to Tania was absolute; he had taken to following her round the house like a small puppy, resenting any attention she gave to Louisa with sulky frowns and the odd explosive rage, which was swiftly forgotten once she concentrated fully on him again. He had inherited all of his father's mercurial changes of mood but with an odd vulnerability, which Tania found quite enchanting. She found herself loving him more and more each day, but was always careful to include Louisa fully in everything they did together, disciplining Emmanuele firmly when she needed to, which was growing less often now he had discovered how far he could go in most situations.

He clambered down from the bed now, his face bright with anticipation. 'Come on, Nana, me want fish.' In the first week she had discovered that the nightly bath was a ritual horror for poor Gilda. Emmanuele hated the water and always refused to co-operate, often having to be held down by force while she hastily washed him, kicking and screaming for all he was worth.

Her sympathies had been all with Emmanuele after the first night; she had recognised the child's fear deep in his eyes as he had approached the bathroom, his bottom lip beginning to tremble long before they had reached the room.

The next day she had driven into the town and let him choose a huge rubber fish, almost as large as himself, which opened its mouth when squeezed tightly and 'drank' water which then was squirted out of brightly coloured fins on either side. Emmanuele had been ecstatic, and within a few days his fear had completely vanished.

As they entered the bathroom she was perturbed to find Enrico sitting, relaxed and smiling, in a large wicker chair close to Louisa, who was gaily splashing and chattering in her high sing-song voice. Gilda was nowhere to be seen.

'Right, young man.' Enrico whisked his small son into his arms, divesting him of his clothes in a manner which spoke of his experience in handling small wriggling bodies. 'Let's see this wonder-fish Louisa has been telling me all about.'

As Tania fetched the fish from the big cupboard just outside the bathroom Emmanuele shrieked with glee, climbing quickly into the bath and holding out his hands imperiously. 'Give me.' His small face was stretched with importance.

Tania looked at him. 'What do you say?'

'Peese.'

'That's better.' She caught Enrico's raised eyebrow and looked at him defensively. 'He's got to learn to say please and thank you.'

'I couldn't agree more.' His lazy voice was approving as he watched Emmanuele squirt water over his screaming sister. 'I was just surprised at the ease with which you seem to have got him under your thumb. I was beginning to despair with Gilda. She means well, but I'm afraid he runs rings round her most of the time.'

He looked at her under his long thick eyelashes. 'Maybe it isn't surprising, though.'

'Oh?' Her voice was stiff. The memory of that afternoon was too vivid for her to relax in his company, and the intimate family feel of the present situation had her stomach muscles tensing in giant knots. She didn't want to be placed in circumstances like these, so close to him and yet so far away.

'You are a very unusual girl, Tania, but I'm sure other men must have told you that.' His voice was gently probing, but she was in no mood for coping with leading questions tonight and, shrugging dismissively, she knelt down by the bath to wash Louisa's hair, keeping any further conversation directed at the children.

The next week flew by. Enrico had left twice as much work for her to type, a good proportion of which had to be completed and sent to him before the weekend, when he was due back for the Christmas holidays. She worked furiously and had finished it all by the Wednesday, growing calmer each day as the hard concentration forced her mind away from destructive self-pity.

In spite of herself, she found she was looking forward to seeing him again. She warned her errant heart to be wary, but as she heard his car draw up on the Friday evening her breath caught tightly in her throat and her pulse raced.

'Hello, there!' She was just leaving the study as he came through the front door, his bronzed face smiling and his brown eyes warm. 'You did a magnificent job with all those reports. Not one mistake! You are definitely improving. I could leave tonight without a qualm.'

'Good.' Her smile was a little shaky. Her heart seemed to have the idea it could leap out of her body, and her legs suddenly felt like water. He looked impossibly handsome as he stood in the doorway, the big overcoat he had on adding to his dark masculinity and his black hair gleaming in the lamplight.

'I'm going to take you out to dinner tonight as a special thank-you, so be ready about eight.'

'I can't.' Her reaction was instinctive, and the smile on his face died as he looked at the panic on her flushed face.

'Why not?' The deep voice was clipped and controlled, but she could see the anger just below the surface in his gleaming eyes.

'The children...and Gilda...they'll expect you to stay with them, and Daisy's prepared something special.'

'I'm sure they will all survive the disappointment.' The sardonic voice was mocking. 'We needn't leave until Emmanuele and Louisa are asleep, and I'm sure they've had their tea by now.' She nodded miserably. 'Well, then, eight sharp.' She looked at him in resigned acceptance; she couldn't fight him and herself. 'I have no intention of making you the dessert on the way home, if that's what's worrying you,' he said grimly, watching her flushed and anxious face as she turned to go towards the kitchen, and his dry, unamused chuckle followed her down the hall as she hurried away, eyes lowered in embarrassment.

An hour later she sat despondently in her bedroom, looking at the meagre array of clothes her open wardrobe door revealed. 'There's just nothing suitable,' she muttered gloomily into the empty room. 'What am I going to do?' The exorbitant rent Mrs Jenkins had charged for the last three years, added to three months of no incoming cash at all, had crippled her finances to bank-ruptcy level, and even with the extremely generous salary that Enrico was paying her it would be some time before solvency was a viable proposition. Enrico had paid Mrs Jenkins the three months' back rent, which, Tania had insisted, against his wishes, she would repay back to him in two instalments after Christmas, and even though her stock of clothes had got dismally low she didn't feel she could replenish it until she was in the black again.

Eventually she decided on a plain long-sleeved white dress in soft wool that she had had for ages but still looked good, its classic lines dateless. After brushing her hair into molten copper she secured it in a high loose knot on the top of her head, allowing a few wispy ten-drils to fall down about her neck, and applied a smudge of dark blue eyeshadow to her eyelids, which turned her eyes into deep azure pools.

'You'll have to do.' She grimaced at her reflection in the mirror, seeing only the slightly snub nose and smat-tering of freckles, and entirely missing the soft beauty of her dark red hair and white skin. The man waiting for her in the shadowed hall missed neither. His black eyes had narrowed briefly at his first sight of her as she descended the stairs, but by the time she reached his side his face was bland and quietly friendly, his deep voice teasing.

'And what time do you call this, Miss Miles? Twenty minutes late!'

She looked at him nervously. He was his usual im-maculate self and she suddenly felt very dowdy and un-attractive, painfully conscious that the dress was four years old and the coat he was holding in his hands for her to slip on had seen better days. She eyed it miserably.

His eyes swept over her tense face in a lightning glance and he suddenly threw the coat on a nearby chair. 'Wait there.' She looked at him in amazement as he took the stairs two at a time, returning after a few seconds with a huge gold cardboard box in his hands. 'I was going to give you this for Christmas but I thought it might come in handy tonight.'

'What is it?' She looked at the package as though it were going to leap out and bite her.

'There's only one way to find out,' he said quietly, placing the box in her hands and standing back a pace as she carefully opened the lid.

'Enrico!' Her gasp of pleasure was quickly followed by a glance of dismay as the beautiful white wool coat the box had held almost slipped from her nerveless fingers, her pale skin flushing painfully. 'I can't accept this.'

'Why not?' His autocratic voice was haughty. 'Of course you can. It's a Christmas present.'

'But it's far too expensive.' Her eyes widened at the label. 'It must have cost hundreds.'

'I don't think it will reduce me to the soup kitchens before we go to Italy.' His voice was faintly mocking. 'I always buy my household Christmas presents. I told you before, while you work for me you become part of my family and are treated accordingly. You needed a warm coat and I liked that one. End of story. Come on, put it on. The table is booked for nine.'

'No, I can't.' She backed away as he took the coat from her. 'It cost too much.'

'Tania!' Her name was an impatient bark, but as he saw the genuine concern in her eyes his face softened, and he shook his head ruefully. 'You really are a very silly little girl.' He made her feel as old as Louisa. 'There is no big deal here; Gilda has something just as nice, and I haven't forgotten Daisy and May. I can afford it and it has given me pleasure; now, please, don't spoil the moment.' He slipped the coat round her shoulders as he spoke, patting her face as though she were six as he turned towards the door. 'Now come on, woman!'

She followed him out into the dark, windy December night with a sinking heart as she pulled the thick soft coat more closely round her slim shape. She was going to have to act as she had never acted before if she was going to get through this evening without betraying her true feelings for him, and she didn't know if she was strong enough. She just didn't know.

CHAPTER SIX

THE restaurant was one Tania had vaguely heard about
but never thought to visit, all subdued lighting, discreet
conversation and superb food in a setting of such luxury
that it quite took her breath away. She was suddenly
enormously thankful for the confidence the beautiful
coat engendered as the attentive waiter gently helped her
out of its sleeves and whisked an embossed menu into
her hands. Enrico was his usual implacable self, totally
unimpressed and slightly sardonic as he glanced round
the scattered tables carefully placed for maximum
privacy.

She raised her eyes fleetingly and then dropped them
again as she met the hard gleaming gaze of a slim dark-
haired woman sitting on the next table. The woman's
eyes had calculated the cost of her dress in one dis-
dainful glance, and then the predatory gaze had moved
on to Enrico, where it had widened appreciatively.

'You look absolutely lovely.' The deep words had her
head snapping up again to meet the dark eyes in which
a small flame seemed to glow for a brief instant.

'I don't feel it.' She tried for a light tone but it came
out more as a plea.

'You don't?' There was genuine amazement in his
voice. 'Well, take it from a connoisseur, my dear, there
isn't a man in this room who wouldn't swap places with
me at this moment in time.' There was no doubt he meant
what he said and, although Tania didn't believe it, she
found it immensely comforting that he did.

'Thank you.' She managed a quick smile. 'I must appear terribly gauche to you. You are used to eating in this sort of place all the time, but I find it a little...'

'Overwhelming?' he finished for her, his face quiet. 'No, you don't appear gauche, Tania. Some women have a natural grace that can carry them into the courts of kings or a beggars' hall with equal charm and sensitivity. Others can have all the money in the world and still remain vulgar and tawdry.' His eyes flickered over the brunette while he spoke, and as she sensed his glance she looked up quickly, her heavily made-up eyes slanting provocatively and the bright red lips pursing into a flirtatious smile that froze as she saw the expression on his face.

Tania looked at him uncertainly as he turned back to her, not sure if he had noticed the little scenario of a few minutes ago and was merely being kind. He reached across the table and lifted her small chin with one finger, his face holding a softly tender expression that turned her legs to jelly. 'You are a very beautiful young lady, and I'm proud to be with you. Now concentrate on me, please, and relax and enjoy yourself. This was meant to be a reward for services over and above the call of duty, not an endurance test.' His smile was very sweet, and pierced her heart like a thorn.

As the courses came and went, with a different wine for each one, she found to her surprise that she really was relishing the unaccustomed extravagance. Enrico was the perfect dinner companion, amusing and attentive, with a dry wit that had her spluttering into her glass more than once. She couldn't have remembered a thing she had eaten afterwards, but every morsel melted in the mouth with calorie-producing deliciousness.

'I could get used to eating here.' Her blue eyes were soft with delight as she glanced up at him, finishing her second helping of dessert. The chocolate and raspberry roulade had melted in her mouth, and as she leant back with a satisfied little sigh she rubbed her stomach ruefully. 'I could turn into something of a glutton, given the opportunity.'

He smiled slowly. 'I doubt it. You would find that after a time eating like this would become an everyday occurrence and, like everything else in life, it would lose its attraction.'

'Do you really mean that?' She had been shocked by the resigned cynicism in his voice and face.

'Of course.' He was suddenly cold and serious-faced, with a hardness in his dark eyes that had not been there all evening.

'Oh, but you are quite wrong, Enrico.' The excellent wine had mellowed her tongue and she found herself leaning forward earnestly as she caught hold of one of his hands in her own. 'Life is a wonderful, exciting gift and not to be wasted, even for a moment. There are so many things that can thrill my heart so that I want to shout or sing—a beautiful sunset, or the sight of a small puppy stumbling along on fat little legs. The thought of Christmas with its own special magic, the smell of turkey and plum pudding mingling with the fragrance of pine needles and crisp frosty air. Don't you have any secret joys...?' Her eager voice trailed away as she saw his face twisted into a harsh mask of pain and contempt with a curious vulnerability in the black eyes that reminded her suddenly of Emmanuele.

'You are talking like a child.' His voice was cruel. 'Life is not a primrose path along which one may wander aimlessly. Life is made up of obligations and responsibilities, of having to reach decisions which may be hard or difficult but, when necessary...' He shrugged wearily. 'There is no escape from them. Sometimes, when it is too late, much, much too late, you realise that the decision you made, in all honesty, has perhaps destroyed someone else's life. That is what living is all about, Tania. Not some airy-fairy wonderland where it's all sweetness and light.'

'I didn't mean that. You know I didn't.' She looked at him despairingly, her eyes huge with hurt. 'I know life can be hard; there isn't a day that goes by when I don't wonder how Melanie is and if she is happy. I hate to think she might be wondering about me too, perhaps even thinking I've abandoned her and that I didn't care.' She took a deep breath, her voice wobbly. 'But if you dwell on dark consuming thoughts you become what they are; they sap the essence of life more successfully than any disease. You must rise above——'

'Stop it!' His deep voice was low but with a piercing intensity that chilled her heart. 'These meaningless platitudes might be all right for you but they mean nothing to me. What do you know of real pain? Have you ever watched anyone you love die? Watched their life-blood slowly seep from their body in a red tide that is unstoppable?'

She stared at him, frozen into a white statue, realising he was talking about Catalina, his wife.

'Do you know how it feels to realise you have murdered the one person in the world who loves you beyond anything you are able to feel? To have them thank you for their death . . . ?' His voice cracked and he ran a hand quickly over his face, his eyes dark, haunted pools of misery.

'You didn't murder her.' She didn't stop to think about what she was saying; her one desire was to bring some relief to the tormented face in front of her. 'It was a million to one chance that your wife would die like that. You had no way of knowing.'

He looked at her sharply, his face straightening into proud autocratic lines that hardened into deep grooves. 'What do you know of it?' His voice was icy.

'Just a little...' Her voice trailed away at the rage in his gleaming eyes.

'Just a little too much.' The cold voice was scathing. 'You are like all of your sex, Tania, ferreting out juicy titbits to savour and gloat over.'

'It wasn't like that,' she protested faintly, her head swimming. How had all this happened? One moment they had been having a friendly relaxed meal, the next——

'Really?' There was a wealth of scorn in the disbelieving tones. 'I'm unconvinced, but I think you would be most ill-advised to venture an opinion on something you know nothing about. My wife made the mistake of loving me, and because of that she paid with her life. It's as simple as that.'

'No, it's not——'

'Don't, Tania. On this subject alone don't argue with me or I will do or say something we will both regret.' He looked at her as though he loathed her, and she shrank from his gaze and the agony it contained. 'We married because it was advantageous to both our families and we had known and liked each other from childhood. What I felt for her was something akin to love for a sister and I thought her love for me was the same. I had sown all my wild oats and was ready to settle down; I had never met a woman I liked more than

Catalina, so it seemed a satisfactory arrangement. In the arrogance of youth I had even shared my romances with her, asked her advice on occasions. When I think now of the pain that must have caused her...' He paused.

'But you loved her; she became your wife.' She was staring at him in horror, unable to keep the shock from whitening her face.

'Haven't you listened to a word I've said?' His voice was a sharp bark. 'I didn't love her, Tania, not in the way a man is supposed to love the woman he marries, and she knew, she knew.' He shook his head slightly. 'After we were married she seemed to want children quickly, and Louisa was born within eighteen months. Catalina was terribly disappointed she hadn't presented me with a son, although I had no preference.' He shrugged slowly. 'She was unable to accept that. It was as though she was driven by a need to be the perfect wife. I think she must have thought that then I would love her as I should. I didn't understand at the time and I wasn't as patient as I could have been.'

He took a sip of wine and held the glass in his hands, running one brown finger round the top of the crystal goblet, his eyes far away in the past.

'When she knew she was going to have another child she was ecstatic, and things were fine again. I promised to be present at this birth—I had been out of the country on business when Louisa was born a month early. It seemed terribly important to her that I was there this time, almost as though she had had a premonition... Anyway, the rest, as they say, is history.'

'But she wanted to be your wife,' Tania said quietly, her eyes soft with pity. 'She had obviously loved you for years, and you gave her the only thing she really wanted.'

'She really wanted to live.' His voice was wretched. 'She was twenty-nine—*twenty-nine*, Tania. Young and beautiful with the rest of her life before her. If she hadn't married me she would still be alive now. She loved me too much and it killed her.'

'That's ridiculous.' Tania's voice was firmer, and her eyes locked with his. 'You gave her four years of happiness instead of gnawing frustration and empty dreams.'

'You don't understand.' His voice was weary. 'How can you possibly understand? I was incapable of giving my heart to her; I don't even know if I have one to give. She would have met someone else who could have loved her as she deserved to be loved.'

'It wouldn't have made any difference.' Tania's voice was inflexible. 'If she had met this imaginary person he wouldn't have been you. She was happy to be your wife and she accepted that you loved her as you did. It was enough for her. She chose for it to be that way. No one held a gun to her head. You can't choose who you fall in love with; it just happens.'

'Not to me.' His voice was cold steel. 'If I could have loved any woman it would have been her. The other women I've known were mere shadows beside her, full of inconsistency and greed and trickery. The female sex is not capable of deep emotion.'

'That's not true.' Tania forced her voice to remain cool and quiet, although her face burned with angry colour and she clenched her hands under the concealing table-cloth. 'Just because you've never met anyone you could love——'

'Love!' His face was tight with scorn. 'What is love? A mere figment of poets' imaginations. I don't believe in love. I have never yet met a woman who was worth that much,' he snapped his fingers dismissively, 'besides my wife. The irony of it all is that I didn't value what I had until it was too late.'

'If she had lived would you have loved her as she loved you, then?' Tania knew he would probably hate her for saying it, but she had to make him face what he was suggesting. 'Could you have manufactured such emotion?'

'How dare you?' His face was dark and furious, and his voice lashed out at her like a striking cobra, although there was a stunned, stricken look in his tormented eyes that told her her words had hit home. 'How dare you talk to me like this?'

'I'm sorry.' She lowered her eyes, her throat constricting in helpless misery. She knew she had just shattered any faint hope she had had for the future. No one liked to be confronted by the truth when it was painful, and it was clearly agonising for him, by the bewildered shock in his dark eyes.

They drank their coffee in silence, Tania feeling as though every mouthful was going to choke her. Enrico's face was as black as thunder, and dark red burnt under his high cheekbones, speaking of violent suppressed rage.

'You have finished?' His voice was cold and curt, and she nodded sadly as he gestured for the bill. The evening had turned to ashes and suddenly the light talk and frivolous company around them seemed like a macabre mockery.

She tried to reach him just once in the car on the journey home. 'Enrico?' His face was set in iron and didn't respond to her soft voice by so much as a flicker of an eyelash. 'Let me explain, please. I know Catalina——'

'Don't speak her name! I never want to hear her name on your lips again.' His voice was like a whiplash cutting

through the night air and branding her with its hate.
'The subject is closed.'

She huddled further into her seat, pulling the soft folds
of the coat more closely around her chilled body, feeling
as though she would never be warm again. He saw the
gesture and turned the car heater full on, but no amount
of warm air could reach through the bleak, raw cold
that was generated from somewhere deep in her flesh.

This was the end. Her whole being cried out against
what her mind was telling her, but after tonight a working
relationship between them would be impossible. He
couldn't even bear to look at her.

It seemed as though every light in the house was
burning as they pulled into the drive, the icy wind
whipping the long bare branches of the oak trees into
swaying motion against the background of the clear, cold
moonlit sky.

'I hope there's nothing wrong.' Tania's words were a
faint murmur, but Enrico nodded sharply in reply, a look
of concern driving the harshness briefly from his mouth.
He brought the car to an abrupt halt and had opened
the door even before the engine had died.

'Enrico, darling.' The cool, cultured female voice met
them as they entered the warmth of the hall, and Tania's
startled eyes were drawn to the doorway of the drawing-
room, where a tall, beautiful blonde woman was
standing, her lovely face rueful. 'Have I arrived at a bad
moment?' The slanted hazel eyes flicked once over
Tania's flushed face and then returned to the tall man
in front of her.

'Selina.' Enrico's voice was warm and he moved to
her side immediately, putting a casual arm round her
waist as he turned to introduce her to Tania. 'This is
Tania Miles. Tania, meet Lady Matheton.'

'Call me Selina,' the woman said graciously, holding out a smooth white hand to be shaken. 'Everyone does.'

'How do you do?' If anything further had been required to complete the disastrous evening Tania had the feeling she was now looking at it. The woman in front of her was every inch an aristocrat, from the top of her smooth ash-blonde head to the tips of her small immaculately shod feet. She was quite breathtakingly lovely, with a beauty that was entirely natural, smooth clear skin, large green- and brown-flecked eyes and a warm friendly smile.

'So you are the wonder-girl Enrico has been telling me about.' The voice was entirely without guile, and as Tania smiled back nervously Selina continued, 'You have helped him out of the most ghastly fix, Tania. I'm afraid I was no assistance at all—in fact, I think I created more problems than I solved.' She turned to Enrico with a small apologetic grimace, and he answered by pulling her closer into his side, his dark face soft and teasing.

'The joy of your presence far exceeded any difficulties,' he drawled with mocking laughter, and she tapped him on the cheek playfully.

'That wasn't what you said when I missed a vital chunk of dictation out of that terribly important report.' She turned to Tania with a wry smile. 'I quote, "What the hell did they teach you in that damn public school?" End of quote.'

'You promised me you wouldn't mention that again.' Enrico pulled her arm through his and prepared to lead her into the drawing-room. It was clear that he had completely forgotten Tania's existence, but Selina turned back to her with a warm smile and a quick questioning glance at Enrico.

'I've enjoyed meeting you, Tania. I hope we will see more of each other over the weekend.'

Enrico took the hint Selina had made and also spoke to her, his voice cold and stiff. 'Goodnight, Tania. Thank you again for all your hard work.' It was clear he had neither forgotten nor forgiven her earlier words, and, flushed with humiliation, she responded with unconscious pride, her chin high and her eyes bright.

'Goodnight, Mr Meliora. Thank you for the meal; it was most enjoyable.' Her voice was brittle and high, and, as her eyes left his face and met the puzzled ones of the woman held in his arm, she smiled bravely. 'Goodnight, Selina.' She didn't trust her voice to say any more and turned swiftly, walking quickly with a straight back towards the stairs, slumping only when she heard the door behind her shut with a loud click just after a long, low feminine giggle had reached her ears.

The next two days were forty-eight hours of subtle torment for Tania. Enrico ignored her almost completely and seemed to delight himself in Selina's company to the exclusion of everyone else, even shutting the children out of their charmed twosome.

When the placid Gilda grew perturbed after Enrico had made no effort to see the children all day Tania felt immense relief that it wasn't all in her imagination. She had begun to feel neurotic. When it was the children's bedtime he gave them a cursory kiss, his expression forbidding when Emmanuele tried to climb on his lap.

'Sleep, Emmanuele.'

The little boy looked up into his father's face; evidently what he saw there made his lower lip tremble, and Gilda caught him round the waist, lifting him down with a muttered admonition.

'I will see you in the morning.' Enrico's harsh face softened as Gilda led his son away, Louisa giving a little wave from the doorway, where she stood with Tania. 'We will all go for a walk in the hills. You would like that, yes?' Emmanuele nodded solemnly, his round brown eyes fastening on Selina, who was sitting by his father's side. There was bright active dislike in their dark depths.

'Lina comin' too?' The query clearly wasn't intended as an invitation, and Enrico's face hardened again, his eyes growing stormy as he looked at the two women standing behind the children in the doorway. It was obvious he blamed them for his son's attitude.

'What does the *signore* expect?' It was the first time Tania had ever heard Gilda criticise Enrico in even the smallest way, and she looked at the Italian woman in surprise as they climbed the stairs with the fretful children. 'He acting strange.' Gilda shook her head despondently. 'Lady Matheton, it not her fault.'

'Have you met her before?' Tania's voice was a little unsteady. There had been cold rage in those dark eyes as they had met hers for a brief moment over the children's heads, and another emotion she couldn't quite define.

'*Sì.*' Gilda nodded slowly. 'Many times. They old friends. She come to Italy on *festa*—how you say, the holiday? She stay with the *signore* and his wife. Catalina and Lady Matheton, they go to the same school in Switzerland. To be finished off?'

'A finishing-school; yes, I see.' Gilda's words had explained the slightly bewildered expression she had caught on Selina's face once or twice that day, a mixture of confusion, sadness and faint unease.

'Lady Matheton, she like the *signore* very much.' Gilda's eyes were sharp with knowledge. 'She always does, but perhaps he now like her too? But he should not forget the *bambini*. Is not right. The *bambini*, they will not like this.'

Gilda's words were confirmed later the next day. Tania had made an excuse not to accompany the others on their walk after Sunday lunch, and was reading quietly in her room when she heard them return earlier than she had expected. The afternoon sky was a brilliant silver blue, the cold December sun a dazzling shining ball in the pearly expanse. It was a perfect winter's day, and she had thought they would stay out until darkness forced them home.

It was only seconds later that a sharp loud knock sounded on her bedroom door, making her jump. 'Come in.' Her voice quavered slightly—there was only one person in this household who would rap the door with such hostility.

'I want a word in private with you.' Enrico stood, dark and furious, just inside the door as she uncurled herself from the bed, her blue eyes apprehensive.

'Yes?'

He kicked the door shut with his foot, his eyes never leaving her face for a moment. 'What have you been telling Emmanuele?'

'Sorry?' She stared at him uncomprehendingly, flinching as he gave a sudden harsh bark of a laugh.

'And don't look like that. It won't work with me. I've seen too many women lie with big eyes wide open and faces as pure as the driven snow.'

'I don't know what you are talking about,' she said coldly, stung and hurt by the heavy contempt in his blazing voice. 'If you have got something to say then say it.'

'Oh, I intend to.' He moved a pace closer to her, his eyes glittering. 'My son informed us all this afternoon that you are going to be his new *mamma*.'

'I don't believe it.'

'Oh, you don't believe it.' His eyes narrowed at the genuine amazement in her shaking voice. 'He dropped this little bombshell in Selina's ear as she picked him up to carry him over a small stream. Needless to say, more than one of us ended up with wet feet.'

'I have no idea why he should say a thing like that. You surely don't think...?' She stopped, horrified by the naked scorn in his face.

'I don't think what? That you are indoctrinating my children with some sort of subtle feminine persuasion? But why should I think that, Tania? What have you possibly got to gain, after all?' The words were bitingly sarcastic, and the caustic insult caused the blood to drain from her face, leaving her white and sick with pain.

'Well?' He took a step nearer, a red glow deep in his eyes. 'What have you got to say?'

She backed away from him and then stopped suddenly as a wild hot rage as great as his own began to put fire in her limbs and loosen her tongue. 'What have I got to say?' She almost spat the words into his bitter face. 'Nothing. I have nothing to say to you. I never want to set eyes on you again. I will not lower myself to defend such a ridiculous suggestion. I didn't want to come here in the first place and how right I was!'

'You deny you have intimated to Emmanuele you could be his stepmother?'

'How dare you?' In her anger she took a step towards him, bringing her within inches of his glowering face. 'You are the last person on this earth I would ever marry, a twisted, dried-up shell of a man like you!' In her agony all she wanted to do was to hurt him the way he had hurt her, to pierce the rigid armour he kept in place round his heart, to wound and destroy. 'I hate you. I've always hated you. There is not one spark of normal human emotion in your whole body.'

'Really?' As her rage grew it seemed to give him greater control over his own anger, and he crossed his arms in front of him, leaning back nonchalantly against the wall, his glittering black eyes the only live things in a face that was as white as a sheet. 'I'm not normal?'

'No, you're not.' She clenched her hands into tight fists by her side to stop their shaking, which was reflected in the whole of her slight frame. 'If Catalina could see you now she would utterly despise you.'

As she spoke the words she knew she had gone too far, but the same force that was driving him had taken hold of her. The furnace that had been glowing behind the dark eyes suddenly burst forth in savage, brutal heat, and he caught hold of her arm in a bruising grip as his teeth drew back from his lips in a snarl.

'I told you before not to mention her name again. You are not worthy to speak it.'

'Oh, yes, I am.' She was beyond fear now, her eyes flashing with a fire that matched his. 'You can think what you like of me, but I know what I am.'

'So do I.' With one movement he jerked her violently into his arms so she landed against his hard chest with a thud. 'I know exactly what you are.' As he lowered his head she began to fight him, tearing at his arms like a small wild animal caught in a trap, her whole body intent on escape. He waited until she was utterly spent and then lowered his head again, taking possession of her lips in a deep burning kiss that had her struggling weakly again, almost on the verge of fainting.

She had expected his mouth to be punishing, but instead there was a slow persuasive charm in the firm warm lips that was taking all the breath from her body, leaving her trembling and frightened as she strove desperately to hold on to her rage and block the assault on her senses.

He began to mould her against the dominance of his flesh, kissing her until all fear and apprehension was washed away in a hot flood of scorching excitement that had her skin burning in feverish anticipation. With a thrill of horror she heard herself sobbing his name against his lips and could feel the evidence of his desire hard against her softness. She couldn't resist him. Her love was a snare with big steel jaws that was holding her in a crushing grip.

His hands moved caressingly over her back, stroking the tense muscles into aching submission before they moved under her jumper and round to the soft fullness of her breasts. As she felt his fingers gently explore the rounded curves she quivered uncontrollably, a piercing sweetness invading her shattered senses.

'No man has ever touched you like this before.' His voice was thick and husky with a trace of triumph in its depths as he dropped fleeting kisses on her upturned face and closed eyelids. 'So fierce and gentle, so young...'

It was as if his voice brought him back to normality, because he straightened suddenly, pulling the air deep into his lungs as he pushed her from him.

'So you hate me, do you?' There was a strange look in his eyes, as though he was forcing himself back into the role of aggressor, and his hands shook slightly as he thrust them into his trouser pockets. 'This dried-up shell that can have you forgetting all your inhibitions within minutes?'

She stared at him with wide eyes, frozen to the spot as a slow chill trickled down her spine. He waited a moment for her to speak and then shrugged as his dark eyes narrowed into cold slits.

'I hope you've learnt your lesson.'

'What lesson is that?' A red tide of hot colour singed her pale cheeks as she remained perfectly still in front of him.

His face hardened into a cruel uninterested mask as his eyes swept her from head to toe. 'That I can take you or leave you, my dear, whereas you...' He paused insultingly. 'Do I have to spell it out?'

A numbness had crept over her as though in preparation for his words, and she was able to lift her head proudly to stare him straight in his mocking eyes. 'I can leave you.' Her voice had a dead sound to it. 'I can leave you this very day.'

'And are you going to?' It was as though he was taking some perverse pleasure from her flight.

'Yes, I am.' She was beyond thinking, all feeling gone in an anaesthetising dullness that had paralysed her mind.

'Well, I would wait until tomorrow.' He looked at her with expressionless eyes. 'It's growing dark outside.'

He left, silently closing the door behind him, and she sank down on the bed with a small bewildered sigh. She would go home. The thought of her parents' rambling old house with its chipped paintwork and untidy garden was suddenly piercingly precious, and as she pictured them in her mind the tears began to flow, not in a healing flood but a wild torrent of despair that rent her body in two.

CHAPTER SEVEN

THE light knock on Tania's bedroom door brought her instantly out of the restless doze she had fallen into, and as she glanced at the small clock by her bed she realised with a start of surprise that it was three o'clock in the morning. She hadn't left her room after Enrico had gone, and no one had come near her. She didn't know what he had said to the others and she didn't care.

'Yes?' She switched her bedside lamp on as the door opened, and was amazed to see the tall, slim form of Selina standing in the doorway, a worried frown wrinkling her lovely face, a blue silk robe loosely knotted over matching pyjamas.

'I'm sorry to disturb you, Tania.' The hazel eyes flicked to the half-packed suitcase in the corner of the room, and as Tania followed her gaze Selina's eyes widened with puzzlement. 'You aren't leaving?'

'Yes, I'm leaving.' Tania's voice was cool and unemotional, although she felt sick inside. Surely Selina hadn't come to gloat? She hadn't attributed such unkindness to her.

'But why?' As Tania made no answer Selina's eyes narrowed in dismay and a slight flush tinged her pale skin. 'Not because of me?'

'Not exactly.' Tania stared at the other woman warily as she moved towards her to sit on the side of the bed. 'What do you want?'

'Emmanuele is not well and he's asking for you, but that can wait a moment.' Selina looked her full in the

face, and Tania's heart sank a little further as she saw
that the early hour had not diminished Selina's beauty
by one iota. 'Why are you leaving?' she asked again. 'I
thought you were happy here.'

'I have my reasons,' Tania answered quietly. 'What is
wrong with Emmanuele?'

Selina brushed aside her question with a small wave
of her hand and spoke urgently, her voice soft and intense. 'Have you argued with Enrico?'

Tania moved restlessly, and Selina surprised her still
further by reaching out and taking her hand in a warm
clasp. 'I'm not your enemy, Tania. Please believe that.'

'Please, Selina...' Tania's eyes dropped in embarrassment. 'I don't think——'

'There is absolutely nothing between Enrico and me
except friendship, Tania.' As her eyes snapped up to meet
the other woman's she saw a wealth of sadness reflected
in them. 'I won't deny I have wished many times for
more, but there it is...' She shrugged slowly. 'He is not
interested in that way. I thought perhaps when Catalina
died that there was a chance, but...' She turned away.
'It's for the best. I've met someone else recently who
loves me very much.'

'I'm sorry, Selina.' Tania's face was fiery red. 'I had
no idea.'

'I'm not surprised.' Selina's voice was gentle. 'If I had
been in your place this weekend I would have been
thinking all sorts of things.'

'It doesn't make any difference to that anyway.' Tania
gestured to the suitcase despondently. 'I've told Enrico
I'm leaving and I think he's quite pleased.' She half
choked on the last word and Selina shot her a swift in-
tuitive glance.

'I wouldn't have put you down for the sort of person who runs when things get a little tough.'

Tania looked at her in amazement, stunned by the quiet, troubled voice. 'I don't know what you mean.'

'I think you do.' Selina nodded her head slowly. 'I have no idea what has transpired between you and Enrico, but one thing I do know: in all the time we have been friends I have never seen him look at a woman the way he looks at you, Tania, and that includes Catalina.'

'You've got this all wrong.' Tania's face glowed with soft colour and her eyes were anguished. 'I think he positively dislikes me.'

'Don't you believe it,' Selina said briskly. 'He is not a man to give his heart lightly, especially after Catalina's death. You know he blames himself for that?' Tania nodded. 'Quite unnecessarily so, of course. Nevertheless, he seems intent on punishing himself indefinitely.'

'Does he know you have met someone else?' Tania asked hesitantly, and Selina gave a small humourless laugh.

'Oh, yes, he introduced me to Philippe, as it happens. We met at Louisa's third birthday party nearly a year ago. Philippe is an old friend of the family.' She looked at Tania soberly. 'If you are looking for an explanation for this weekend I can give you one. It isn't that he's falling in love with me, Tania. He has never given me any hope in that direction. I've always known I'm just Catalina's friend to him. This is the first time I've known a woman get under his skin and for him to behave so badly. Draw your own conclusions.'

'I'm sorry, Selina. I know you mean well, but you don't understand.' Tania's voice was weary. 'In any case, I shall leave in the morning. I've told him now and it's all agreed.'

'Don't let pride stand in your way,' Selina said softly. 'You'll regret it for the rest of your life if you do.'

'Would you beg to be allowed to stay?' Tania looked straight into the other woman's eyes, and after a long moment Selina's gaze dropped. 'No, I thought not, and neither will I. Thank you for trying, Selina; I'll never forget it. Now...' her voice became brisk '...what's wrong with Emmanuele?'

If it hadn't been for the circumstances Tania could have smiled at the sight that met her eyes as she and Selina reached the children's room. Gone was the cold, harsh, autocratic man of a few hours before, and in his place was a distraught father, carrying his small son's limp body in his arms as he paced the floor, his eyes frantic and his big body as tense as a steel rod.

'Nana.' Emmanuele's voice was as listless as his body and the plump arms that reached out towards her drooped instantly.

'Have you called the doctor?' Tania avoided looking directly at Enrico while she spoke, taking Emmanuele in her arms as he began to murmur her name, big tears running down his chubby little cheeks.

'Of course,' Enrico answered. 'Louisa woke Gilda half an hour ago because Emmanuele was crying, and once I'd felt how hot he was I called immediately.' His voice was quiet but there was a deep throb of worry in its depths, and he was grim-faced.

'Take his pyjamas and dressing-gown off, Gilda.' Tania laid the tiny body in his cot. 'Would you get some lukewarm water, Selina, and a soft sponge?'

'Of course.' Selina sped away immediately, pulling her robe tighter around her as she left.

'What are you doing?' Enrico's voice was harsh with protest as Tania and Gilda stripped the small figure of all his clothes.

'He's burning up. We've got to bring the temperature down or he'll have a convulsion. Sit by the cot and talk to him, Enrico. Try and calm him down.' With something akin to amazement in his eyes, Enrico did just as she asked, taking Emmanuele's plump little hands in his own and talking to him in sing-song Italian.

'What do you think is the matter?' Selina whispered to Tania as they took turns in sponging the small figure down. 'He's so hot.'

'It looks like German measles to me,' Tania murmured in reply, trying to ignore Enrico's dark eyes fixed on her face as he still held his son's hands in his own large ones. 'Rob, my younger brother, had a rash like this when he was about three, and his temperature shot sky-high. Normally German measles can come and go without anyone even noticing, but occasionally a child reacts badly with a high temperature. He'll probably be as right as rain in a couple of days, but the temperature is the thing to worry about at the moment. The drink I just gave him contained junior paracetamol, so that might help too.'

The doctor more or less confirmed her words when he eventually came, congratulating Tania on her handling of the situation. 'So many people try and wrap them up like mummies when they've got a temperature,' he said soberly. 'Worst thing you can do, worst thing.' Tania didn't dare look at Enrico standing quietly by the door.

It was a long night. Emmanuele got distressed every time Tania was out of his sight for a moment, so at first light, when he was cooler, she took him into her room, lying him on top of the bed with a light covering and balancing precariously on the far side, pulling the duvet round her like a cocoon.

He went to sleep almost immediately, looking impossibly angelic with his small face flushed and black curls damp, one small arm hooked firmly round his teddy bear. Her heart wrenched with love as she lay gazing at the tiny inert figure curled, facing her, under the thin sheet. She would find it almost as difficult to leave the children as she would their father.

The dawn chorus reached a crescendo in the big copper beech outside her window and gradually died away as the pale wintry sun rose in an arctic sky. She heard the milkman come and go, and gradually her racing mind slowed down as her eyelids drooped in sleep. She was unaware of a tall dark presence standing quietly by the bed, looking at the sleeping child and woman for endless minutes, then gathering a small bundle in his arms as he silently left the room.

'Tania.' She woke to a gentle hand stroking stray tendrils of hair from her face, and opened dazed blue eyes to find Enrico's bronzed face a few inches from her own. 'Good morning, Nurse.' The rich deep voice was warm and tender with some emotion she couldn't recognise in its depths.

'Oh! What's the time?' She struggled to sit up, feeling light-headed and bewildered, and then slid promptly back down under the covers as she realised her only protection from those knowing black eyes was the thin silk of her nightie.

'Spoilsport.' His voice was mocking and the dark face was alight with laughter.

'Emmanuele? Where is he?' As her mind came fully out of sleep she glanced round the room agitatedly. 'I must have fallen asleep.'

'Emmanuele's fine. His temperature is down and he
seems to be suffering no ill-effects, thanks mainly to you,
I might add.'

She glanced into the face looking at her so intently
and then hastily lowered her eyes. 'I didn't do anything,'
she protested weakly as she let her hair fall about her
hot cheeks in a protecting veil.

'Well, you certainly did a darn sight more than the
rest of us.' He straightened up and moved across to the
window, pulling the curtain aside to reveal soft fat flakes
of snow falling from a laden sky. 'I should have known
to keep him cool. I don't know what I was thinking of.
Unfortunately Gilda is no help in that sort of
emergency—she's had no real training, and she does tend
to go to pieces.' He turned back to her as he spoke, se-
curing both curtains in the thick velvet loops provided
so that the soft glow from the white sky filled the room.

'How long has it been snowing?' Tania couldn't keep
the thrill of pleasure from her voice.

'Is snow another of your pet joys?' He smiled a slow,
lazy smile that crinkled the corners of his eyes and almost
stopped her heart from beating. 'I might have known.
Everyone else bemoans blocked roads and inconvenient
delays while you cheerfully build a snowman. About
right?'

She looked at him warily, her eyes shadowed with uncertainty, and as he caught her expression he moved
swiftly to her side again, his face tender. 'I'm not criti-
cising, Tania, merely envious.' His face was oddly
wistful. 'I used to feel the way you do once, a long, long
time ago, but then life got in the way and I lost the gift
that children take for granted of looking at each new
day as an enchanted opportunity, full of possibilities.'

He looked again at the window. 'Snow became just another problem.'

'That's very sad,' she said quietly and he nodded slowly, his eyes lost in inner thoughts that brought the familiar chill to his handsome face.

'Tea.' He came out of his reverie suddenly and smiled at her, pointing to a steaming cup at the side of the bed. 'I brought you a cup of tea.'

'Thank you.' She felt acutely embarrassed as his eyes rested on the suitcases in the corner of the room, but he said nothing, wandering to the window again and standing with his back to her as she drank the hot tea.

'Emmanuele will be broken-hearted if you leave.' She almost dropped the cup on the bedspread as his voice, cold and hard, crackled into the uneasy silence.

'He's only a baby. He will forget me in a couple of days,' she said softly.

'Don't you believe it. He is a Meliora male—he doesn't give his heart easily.' His back was still to her and she looked at his broad figure despairingly. What did he want of her? She couldn't continue working for him, living in the same house, when he had told her so explicitly that he wanted her gone. She remembered the look on his face at the restaurant and again the night before; it had been burning with scorn, contempt and an even stronger emotion, which she had felt to be hate. For every step she took that brought her closer to understanding this complex man, he made her take two back. 'You are leaving today?' The harsh voice vibrated along her nerve-endings, causing her to wince in pain.

'I think it's best,' she said shakily. If only he would ask her to stay, give some indication that he didn't totally despise her.

'Would you be prepared to wait until after Christmas, when we return from Italy?' He turned to face her, a strange shuttered expression on his dark face. 'It would be better for Emmanuele, as he expects you to come—Louisa too. All the arrangements have been made, and it would save a lot of laborious explanations.

For a moment, as she looked into the cool, unreadable face, she wished with all her might she could find it in herself to hate this dark foreign stranger with his cold mind and even colder heart. He seemed to be made of stone.

She looked at him, searching for even a glimmer of warmth in his watchful eyes, but there was nothing. She sighed wearily. 'I suppose so, if you think it's best. I don't want to upset the children's Christmas.' She rubbed her hand tiredly across her face as she spoke, missing the sudden deep heat that blazed for a second in the backs of his eyes.

'Good.' His voice was curt and matter-of-fact. 'That's settled, then. We'll go on with the plans as before. You will assist Gilda with the children today? Emmanuele wants you.'

'Yes, all right.' She glanced at him suddenly as a thought struck her. 'Is Selina still here? She was very good last night.'

'Selina has gone back to London.' His voice held that thread of impatience she was learning to recognise. It meant his razor-sharp mind had moved on to new territory. 'She sends her best wishes and hopes to see you again soon.'

'Oh.' Her voice was small. She had hoped for a further talk with Selina to continue their conversation of the night before.

'She waited as long as she could to say goodbye personally, but when it started to snow we thought it best not to delay.'

'Of course.'

He gave her another long considering glance as he left the room. 'She is very taken with you.'

'Is she?' Tania flushed a warm pink. 'I liked her too.'

'Hmm.' His dark eyes gleamed. 'I got the impression you were avoiding her at one point. You didn't join us on the walk.'

'Did you?' She opened her eyes very wide. 'I can't think why you would have thought that. *Selina's* company is most acceptable.'

The small dry chuckle he gave as he left the room told her her parting shot had hit its target.

Starry flakes of snow were still falling lightly the next day. The country lanes and bare trees had been transformed into a winter wonderland of cold white beauty, the dry stone walls and low hedgerows taking on a feathery brilliance all of their own. The blizzard conditions of the day before had vanished, and, although the air was crisp and cold, it was inviting.

'Who's going to help me build a snowman?' asked Tania at breakfast as they all sat in cosy harmony round the big table, while a huge crackling fire in the ornate fireplace sent a bright cascade of golden sparks up the chimney.

'Me! Me!' Louisa wriggled her small body in rapt contemplation of Tania, and Emmanuele copied her, nearly falling off his chair, not at all sure what all the excitement was about but keen not to miss anything.

'Will you come, *Papà*?' Louisa's small face was hopeful, and as Tania saw the refusal forming on Enrico's firm mouth she intervened quickly.

'Of course he will. *Papà* would love to spend a day with his two favourite people.'

'Of course I will, Louisa.' Enrico's face made it plain she had backed him into a corner. '*Papà* would love to spend a day with his two favourite people.' He repeated her words with cool mockery but it was lost on the children, who jumped up and down with pleasure.

'Come.' Gilda took their hands firmly. 'We must change into suitable clothes, *sì*?'

'Yes, Gilda.' Louisa's voice was resigned, but her eyes were bright with excitement as she and Emmanuele left the room with the Italian woman.

'I think this is the time to strike a bargain.' Enrico's deep voice brought Tania's head springing up to meet his intent gaze across the table.

'A bargain?' She stared at him warily. 'What sort of bargain?'

'I feel our last outing together was not quite as enjoyable for you as it should have been.' His face was carefully bland, but she flushed a bright scarlet as she remembered the disastrous finish to the evening. 'I would like to make amends.'

'That isn't necessary.' She looked down at her plate as she spoke.

'Nevertheless. You were excellent with Emmanuele the other night and I would like to thank you in my own way. We will go out for a meal this evening.'

That was why he wanted to take her out! Out of gratitude for her handling of Emmanuele's illness. For a moment she felt a stab of pain so sharp that it took all her will-power to sit still. 'No, it's all right. You are paying me to take care of the children, after all.' She hadn't meant the words to sound quite so blunt.

'Tania.' He spoke her name so softly that for a moment she thought she had imagined it. She raised her hot face to meet his sombre gaze. 'I worded that very badly and I apologise. I would genuinely like the pleasure of your company tonight. Will you come?'

Put like that, she couldn't refuse, and if she was honest with herself she had to admit she wanted to go with him, anywhere, any time. 'Thank you, yes, I'd love to.'

He smiled slowly, and the smile was so sweet that it wrenched at her heart. 'Good. We will spend the day with the children and then the night will be ours.' He didn't mean anything by his words, but they caused a deep, hard longing so violent in its intensity that she dropped her eyes swiftly again. She would go mad before this was finished.

She was to remember that day for a long time as one of bitter-sweet enchantment filled with magical moments that had her feeling as if her feet had wings. It was almost as though they were a family as they built first a snowman, then a small igloo in the crisp, clean air filled with shouts of glee from the children and deep warm chuckles from Enrico.

She saw a side to him that he had never revealed before, and for the first time he seemed really to relax in her company. Gilda only stood the first ten minutes in the frosty air and then disappeared inside, leaving the four of them to their own devices. His enjoyment of his children was touching, and more than once Tania had a lump in her throat as she watched his sensitive and loving dealings with them. She would have given all she possessed for one day as his wife and their mother, and the knowledge that she was as expendable to him as any other of his employees became an increasingly bitter pill to swallow.

They came indoors finally as the sky became washed with red fire and dusk chilled the air, leaving the results of their labours in proud prominence on the lawns.

As Gilda took the children away for their bath Enrico caught her hand as she went to move to the big staircase. 'I can't remember when I have enjoyed a day more, and it was all thanks to you.'

'Hardly.' She gave a nervous laugh; the touch of his warm hand was not helping her breathing. 'The children were great, though, weren't they? I——'

'It was all thanks to you.' There was a strange look in his eyes, almost torment, as he stared down at her, and for a long moment they stood there, their eyes locked, while time stood still.

The sound of Daisy suddenly breaking into unmelodious song in the kitchen shattered the mood, and with a dry smile he let go of her hand and looked along the hallway. 'I have to admit the thought of an à la carte menu holds a certain attraction after a few days of Daisy's cooking.' His gaze was rueful. 'The phrase "plain but wholesome" has taken on a whole new meaning since I've been here.'

She smiled weakly in reply. His words had reminded her they were going to spend the evening together, and the fluttering in her stomach didn't bode well for the à la carte.

'Can you be ready for seven?'

'That'll be fine.' She escaped to her room quickly, almost falling up the stairs in her haste to leave his presence.

She dressed very carefully that evening. After a day spent in the open air her skin had a dewy bloom to it that cosmetics couldn't enhance, and so she merely brushed a little eyeshadow on her lids and a light coating of mascara on her thick lashes. The dress she had chosen was a plain one in a soft warm gold, and she left her hair loose, stroking her face in a burnished silky cloud, adding long gold earrings, which had been a twenty-first birthday present from her parents, to complete the effect. She wanted to look elegant and older tonight; she needed to feel in control.

The snow was glistening as though it had been scattered with millions of tiny diamonds; Enrico helped her into the car, and she breathed in the clear, frosty air as it touched her face with cold fingers.

'Isn't it lovely to be warm and snug in a little house on wheels when it's so cold outside?' Tania said softly after a few minutes, blissfully uncurling her toes in the warmth of the car heater.

'I think "little house" is a slight exaggeration,' Enrico said caustically as he negotiated a particularly sharp bend where a patch of black ice gleamed dark in the road. 'I hate to put a damper on your spirit, Tania, but you'll have to excuse me if I fail to rise to your heights of enthusiasm over the present weather conditions. I've built a snowman with Emmanuele and Louisa and leapt about like a demented Eskimo all day, but just at the moment this snow is giving me one hell of a headache.'

'Yes, it can be a pig round here,' Tania agreed cheerfully, 'you'll really have to concentrate.'

'Thank you.' The words were full of irony, and after a quick glance at his sardonic face she lapsed into silence, focusing her attention on the pale picture-box world outside the car in an effort to ignore the big, lean body so close to hers. There was something incredibly seductive in his easy mastery of the powerful car, and she

was desperately thankful that he didn't have the power
to look into her mind.

It was just after eight when they reached the small
secluded hotel where Enrico had reserved their table, and
the evening flowed in much the same way as the day had
done. This time there were no confidences to spoil their
enjoyment of the meal, and Tania found herself trying
to savour every moment spent in his company. After
Christmas these memories would have to last her a very
long time.

She slipped on the smooth frozen snow as they left
the hotel, and Enrico's hand shot out to grasp her arm
in a firm grip. 'Thank you.' She laughed slightly as he
walked with her to the car, concentrating on the ice
underfoot and missing the hot glance of burning hunger
that lit the furnace behind his eyes as he gazed at her
bent head.

They were halfway home when thick flakes of snow
began to fall from a dark laden sky, blown into a mad
swirling dance by an icy wind. Enrico swore softly as
his windscreen wipers laboured with their weighty load,
and the car was reduced to crawling along the snow-
packed lanes.

'Will we get home?' Tania looked at him anxiously
as he sat crouched over the wheel, all his energy concentrated on the road ahead.

'Of course.' His tone was calmly reassuring, and Tania
suddenly had the crazy notion that even the elements
wouldn't dare to contradict him now he had spoken. 'You
aren't frightened, are you?'

'Not really.' She glanced at the hard profile shyly. 'Not
with you driving.'

He shot her a swift penetrating glance and then kept
his eyes to the front. 'Really?' His tone was dry. 'I would

have thought, in view of the circumstances in which you joined my household, you wouldn't value my driving ability too highly.'

'That was an accident,' she said firmly. 'It could have happened to anyone. I'm glad you swerved to avoid the fox.'

He smiled lazily, without looking at her flushed face. 'Let's hope we don't meet the same situation tonight. With a passenger in the car I would have to act differently.'

'You'd hit it?' She couldn't keep the note of condemnation out of her voice.

'Of course.' His voice had that metallic ring to it that told her her disapproval had been noted. 'You are my responsibility, and my first consideration must be to ensure your safety.'

'What about your safety?'

He shrugged disdainfully. 'That is my concern.'

'You take your responsibilities seriously, don't you?' She looked at the hard dark profile so close to her. 'Don't you ever want to run through fresh green grass in your bare feet, or take off for the day without warning, or——?'

'We're back to fairy-tales again?' His voice was tight. 'For goodness' sake, Tania, act your age.'

'Why?' She knew she was provoking him but was unable to stop. 'Because you always do? Well, no, you don't actually. You act like someone fifty years older.'

'From your limited knowledge of me, I fail to see that you can make an accurate observation on my character.' His voice was now as cold as the white world outside.

'Huh!' She clenched her hands and bit back the words that were hovering on her lips.

'Huh?' He echoed her exclamation disparagingly. 'What does that mean? Just because I don't have some strange hippy-type approach to life I'm labelled dead meat in that sharp little brain of yours?' His voice was caustic. 'I have various businesses to run, a family; I'm not——'

Now it was her turn to interrupt him. 'But all those things needn't make you so...' she searched for a word to describe how she felt he was '...serious,' she finished weakly as he cut the engine in exasperation and turned to face her, his dark eyes brilliant in the half-light.

'You'll drive me mad, woman.' His voice was a thick whisper. 'We're in the middle of nowhere in the midst of a blizzard and you want to act as my psychiatrist? Why, why does it matter to you?'

She stared, mesmerised, as he lifted his hand and gently stroked her shining hair, following the soft folds down to her throat. She couldn't answer him; her mouth was dry and her heart was pounding. 'Why, Tania?' he asked again, genuine puzzlement in his deep voice.

'You've so much to give, and you seem so...locked into yourself,' she whispered softly in answer.

He said nothing as his hand moved upwards to trace a lingering path over her cheek, forehead, brows. 'So soft.' His voice was husky. 'Such contrasts in one little package.' She was waiting for the moment when he drew her gently to him, the snow coating the windows like a thick white blanket and enclosing them in their own small, private world.

He took her lips with a deep groan, and this kiss was like no other that had gone before, a trembling, terrifying need evident in the hard mouth devouring hers.

'What are you doing to me ... ?' His words were feverish on her lips as their breath mingled. 'I want you, Tania; I want you so badly that I can taste it.'

She was powerless to resist him, her love responding instantly to the hunger in his voice and the hardness of the big male body moulded against her softness. The strength of his body was frightening but thrilling, and her arms moved round the muscled back to pull him even closer to her until she was fitted against him in tantalising harmony.

'Stop me, Tania.' His voice was a harsh plea in the darkness as his hands explored her shaking body. 'Stop me now.' Instead she pulled his head down to hers, covering the hard jaw and firm mouth in tiny burning kisses until with an almost savage movement he took her mouth again in a scorching kiss that had her drowning in shuddering pleasure.

'Enrico, Enrico...' She breathed his name against the taut warm flesh of his throat, unaware she was speaking aloud as she voiced her deepest desires. 'I want to belong to you, to be yours...'

The shock of his rejection was so sudden that for a stunned moment she whimpered his name again into the darkness. At her muttered words he had become still against her, his hands frozen on her body and his mouth numb against her lips. For an endless moment they seemed suspended in space, the silent world outside and a piercing quietness within, and then he moved soundlessly, gently pushing her back into her own seat as he slid back into his own.

They sat without speaking for some moments, Tania staring blankly at the snow-covered windscreen and Enrico with his head resting in his hands on the leather-clad steering-wheel.

'Why didn't you tell me?' His voice was a murmur in the stillness. Her heart stopped breathing; he had guessed how she felt.

'I don't know what you mean.' She stared proudly ahead, her eyes burning with unshed tears and a dull deep ache in her chest. This was the final humiliation and she had brought it on herself.

He glanced at her white face with a pain in his eyes that was as deep as her own. 'I didn't want this, Tania; I can't give you what you need.'

'You don't understand.' Her voice was high and brittle as she desperately sought to salvage a little thread of crushed pride. 'It was just a heat of the moment thing, wasn't it? Nothing important.'

He didn't answer for a moment, and then sighed heavily. 'Yes, of course. Just a momentary weakness.' His voice was full of a desolate sadness and something else she took to be pity.

'We'd better clean the windscreen and get home.' She tried to stop the misery that was turning her whole body into a raging hot inferno coming through in her voice, looking down at her tight-fisted hands in her lap as her hair covered her burning cheeks in a soft protecting veil.

'Yes.' He answered automatically, without moving. 'Tania——'

'Don't.' Her voice shook as she stopped what he was about to say. 'Please take me home.' She cleared her throat as her voice cracked. 'Please.'

He started the engine without another word, his dark face drawn and grim, and as the car purred into life she felt an agony of mind that was more searing than any physical pain. She had gambled everything and lost. There was nothing for her now.

CHAPTER EIGHT

As TANIA stepped off the plane at the Italian airport, holding Louisa tightly by the hand, the first thing she noticed was the cool soft air enveloping her in the shadowed darkness. 'It's not cold.' She lifted surprised eyes to Enrico, who was carrying a tired Emmanuele piggy-back-fashion, and Gilda laughed softly by her side.

'*No, no*, it nice, eh? It get cold, *sì*, but not like your English ice and snow.' She shivered graphically.

Enrico glanced at Tania, his dark eyes unreadable. 'We're in a warm spell at the moment, so make the most of it. It can turn very chilly in the mountains where we will be.'

She nodded silently. Since their evening out together with its disastrous conclusion he had maintained a polite and distant attitude towards her, for which part of her was grateful. The children didn't seem to be aware of any atmosphere, but she had noticed Gilda's puzzled looks of concern, although the Italian woman had tactfully forborne to make any mention of it. Her thoughts skimmed back to the preceding days.

She had woken the next morning, determined to leave that day, but Gilda had informed her at breakfast that Enrico had left earlier to finish some business before the proposed trip. He had obviously withdrawn to give her a breathing-space in which to think, and by the time he had returned two days later she had been composed and dignified, at least externally, intent on finishing her con-

133

tract with him, as arranged, and leaving after Christmas with the minimum of fuss.

'Nana, me want Nana.' Emmanuele was struggling fretfully on his father's back, and Enrico hugged him to his hard chest as he deftly turned him round, his face tender.

'Come on, little one, you'll soon see Pookey.'

'Pookey?' Tania's voice was quizzical, and Louisa piped up by her side, her small face bright and excited.

'That's Emmanuele's baby horse. I've got one too, but mine is grown up and she's called Velvet. I ride her all by myself, and I've only fallen off once.'

'Well, done, darling.' Tania answered automatically, her stomach churning at the thought of the next two weeks. It was bad enough seeing Enrico each day, his handsome face cold and aloof, but having to meet all his relations and friends...

They walked straight through Customs to where their luggage was being loaded in a chauffeur-driven white Mercedes. '*Ciao, Ramone.*' Enrico shook hands with the elderly uniformed driver, who had clicked to attention at first sight of his master, his lined face breaking into a beam of delight as Gilda flung her arms round him in a warm hug. 'Her father,' Enrico explained briefly as he helped Tania into the back of the car.

It was too dark to see any of the countryside through which they were travelling, but the sky was a deep blue-black blanket overhead in which the stars nestled like tiny twinkling crystals, and the small sleeping villages were fascinatingly foreign as they sped through deserted streets.

The big car had been climbing steadily for over an hour when they finally drew into a long pebbled drive through a huge arched entrance surrounded by a high stone wall. Tania was aware of a shadowed figure closing two massive iron gates, and then her breath caught in her throat as she had her first glimpse of Enrico's home.

The house was set on a low hill, sheltered by huge old oak trees and cypress, and surrounded by landscaped gardens, the soft colour of the old brick in magnificent contrast to the foliage. As they drew nearer it seemed as if the old house was ablaze with colour from the light shining from the huge leaded windows and the hundreds of tiny coloured lamps hanging in the surrounding trees.

'Welcome to Casa delle Querce,' Enrico said softly as he turned round from his place next to Ramone to look directly into her wide blue eyes. 'It means Oak Tree House, incidentally—now you know why I was particularly taken with Great Oaks; it resembled home.'

As they drew up outside the mansion she had the fleeting thought that even Great Oaks in all its splendour couldn't compete with this palatial residence. For the first time the enormity of Enrico's wealth and affluence gripped her mind with steel-cold fingers, and the utter foolishness of losing her heart to this handsome, dangerously powerful man numbed her senses as the chauffeur opened the door and helped her alight.

'*Ecco a lei*, Enrico!' The tall, beautifully dressed woman standing in the arched doorway brushed Enrico's cheek in a cool gesture of welcome, her eyes hardening fractionally as he turned towards Tania, standing with the children either side of her at the bottom of the wide marbled steps.

'English, please, Mother. Tania doesn't understand our language.'

The children hadn't rushed to greet their grandmother as Tania had expected, and now they climbed the steps with their hands clasped in hers and their small faces subdued.

'*Buonasera, Nonna*,' they chorused as she patted them lightly on their heads, her dark eyes lingering for a second on Emmanuele's bent head.

'Good evening, my dears.' Her voice was gentle but cool, and the autocratic face that met Tania's nervous gaze had no warmth in its still beautiful features. Enrico's mother must have been at least fifty years old, but looked ten years younger, her smooth skin faintly lined and glowing with health, her brown eyes clear and bright.

'You must be Tania.' She held out her hand with regal formality, and for a moment Tania wasn't sure if she expected her to shake it or kiss it.

'How do you do?'

'When Gilda has put the children to bed, and you have changed and refreshed yourself after the journey, please join us in the main drawing-room for cocktails.' She spoke as one granting a great privilege, and as Tania lifted her eyes from the cold face she saw Enrico's mouth had pulled into a thin harsh line.

'You understand Tania is here as a guest, Mother?' His low voice carried a silky warning that brought a slight flush to the older woman's high sculptured cheekbones.

'Of course, Enrico. You made that perfectly clear.' The cool voice was expressionless, but something in the imperious face chilled Tania's heart as she looked bewilderedly from one to the other.

'Oh, but I didn't expect——'

'Twenty minutes, Tania.' Enrico's deep voice cut in on her faltering murmur of embarrassment. 'Candice will show you to your room and I will come to collect you in twenty minutes.'

She shot him a look of sheer panic as the small smiling maid took her arm to lead her towards the wide curving staircase in the middle of the vast hall, and he met her frightened gaze with a warm smile, his dark eyes kind. 'We'll go along to the children before we go down. Emmanuele will not allow his next instalment of *Wind in the Willows* to be missed.'

She smiled weakly in reply. This was the first time he had shown her any warmth since that awful evening four nights ago and it didn't help. She could keep her errant heart under control while he maintained his distance, and to know his friendliness now was motivated by compassion brought a hot flush of humiliation to her cheeks.

She was sitting straight-backed and tense on the wide soft bed when he knocked exactly twenty minutes later, the overpowering opulence of the sumptuous room adding to the overall feeling of doom. Why had she come? She must have been mad. She had nothing to wear and she was bound to disgrace herself in front of all his relations and friends with their beautiful clothes and cultured talk. Why hadn't she stayed in England? a little inner voice mocked her as she twisted her hands anxiously in her lap. You know why you came, why you always intended to come. You want to be near him at any cost. She sighed dispiritedly. Where was her pride? It had all been burnt up by one glance from those smouldering black eyes.

'Come in.' Her voice shook slightly, and as he opened the door his eyes narrowed on her white face.

'Come on, Tania.' The rich voice was soft. 'Where's all your fighting spirit?' She stared at him with wide eyes, her throat constricting as she took in the black dinner suit and crisp white shirt, the bronzed darkness

of his skin and the leashed power in the big muscled
body that the clothes couldn't hide.

'Do I look all right?' Her wavering voice told him that
the question was a genuine appeal and he answered it
as such, his eyes brilliant with some emotion as he took
in her slim young form in the simple blue evening dress.

'You look fine, absolutely fine, and don't worry, we
won't dress for dinner every night. Mother does tend to
hold to the old traditions, but when I am home I like to
relax a little too.'

She smiled gratefully. 'That's just as well. I've only
got two evening dresses and they are both years old.'

'They don't look it.' His dark eyes took in the thick
silky red hair and smooth white skin, and a small muscle
tightened in his tanned cheek. 'You look quite lovely—
you always do.'

He turned away abruptly and when he next spoke his
voice was cold and harsh again as though he was re-
gretting the intimacy of their conversation. 'Let's go and
see Louisa and Emmanuele, and then I'm afraid you'll
have to run the gauntlet of my assembled family. It won't
be too bad; there's only Mother and a couple of aunts,
along with Camillo, my cousin.' His voice hardened
slightly on his cousin's name and she glanced at him
enquiringly, but the austere dark face revealed nothing.
'The rest of the company will be arriving on Christmas
Eve.'

The evening passed in a rush of jumbled impressions
that churned in her mind later as she lay in bed re-
viewing the last few hours. The dinner had been excellent, served by the little maid Candice and a tall,
serious-faced woman in similar attire. The aunts had
proved to be carbon copies of Enrico's mother,
somewhat dour-faced and haughty, silently eating the

delicious food as course upon course was placed before them.

The only bright spot in the evening had been Camillo, Enrico's cousin. She had been surprised at her first sight of him; he was as fair as Enrico was dark, smooth blond-brown hair worn long into his neck and a pair of wickedly bright blue eyes that seemed alight with amusement the whole night long. She had had the feeling that he found the supercilious attitude of the three older women as hard to take as she did, and he hadn't missed an opportunity for wry comment and outrageous tongue-in-cheek banter. He was probably a couple of years younger than Enrico, she'd thought consideringly, her eyes tight on the handsome face, and then had blushed furiously as she'd realised the deep blue eyes were staring straight at her, sensual warmth glowing in their sapphire depths. She'd turned away abruptly but not before her eyes had caught sight of Enrico, who had been looking at the little episode. The look on his face had frightened her, and she'd kept her eyes on her plate for much of the time after that.

She'd been enormously thankful when after coffee— presented in exquisite tiny gold-rimmed glasses and as thick as treacle—had been served Enrico's mother had turned to her with a tight smile stretching her cold face.

'You look exhausted, my dear,' she said coolly. 'Your duties with the children must have tired you out. Perhaps you would like to retire?' With a flash of intuition Tania understood the reason for the barely concealed antagonism this proud woman had shown her since first setting eyes on her. In his mother's eyes Enrico had unforgivably crossed the master-servant line in asking that Tania be greeted as a guest in his house. Convention had been flouted; Tania was not in her rightful place.

Camillo was looking distinctly uncomfortable and Enrico's face had set into stone, and, sensing that he was about to speak, she answered his mother swiftly, keeping her gaze level and her voice steady, although two spots of bright colour were burning in her high cheekbones. She would not let the Italian woman have it all her own way.

'Thank you, Mrs Meliora, and I must thank you for the warm welcome you have given me. I'm sure you realised I was feeling a little nervous, being in a strange country, and your kindness is very much appreciated.' The cool tone in which she spoke could not have been misunderstood, and as blue eyes clashed with startled brown Enrico's mother recognised and accepted the subtle insult to her hospitality. There was no way she could retaliate and after a long moment she smiled coldly, her eyes as hard as glass but with a faint glimmer of respect in their iron depths that had been absent before.

'Enrico's friends are my friends,' she said stiffly, her voice slightly arrogant. 'I hope you enjoy your short stay with us.'

Tania inclined her head towards the older women without replying and rose gracefully from the table, her movements relaxed and unhurried. Enrico's face was not unfriendly as she wished him goodnight, and Camillo's was positively glowing with roguish delight. She felt a sudden quick moment of affinity with Enrico's cousin— he, at least, was human.

'I will walk you to your room.' Enrico's calm voice brought her head swinging up to his as she smiled at Camillo, and for a second she could have sworn she had surprised a look of some burning emotion glowing deep in those black eyes, but it was gone in an instant as she replied.

'That's not necessary, thank you. I won't get lost.' She smiled to soften her refusal, but he moved to take her arm possessively, his face rigid.

'Nevertheless.'

She knew that tone and capitulated without further argument—she had had enough for one night. 'Goodnight, everyone.' She turned with Enrico to the door as Camillo's rich low voice answered swiftly.

'Goodnight, Tania. I will see you tomorrow.'

The next morning she awoke to Candice drawing back the fine silk drapes from the latticed windows, the small maid's face bright and smiling as she met Tania's confused gaze.

'Good morning, *signorina*.' She gave a little curtsy as she spoke. 'I bring the breakfast for you. *Si?*'

'Thank you, Candice.' Tania struggled up in the wide soft bed as she glanced around the magnificent room, and Candice immediately placed a loaded tray on her lap.

'Is good, eh?'

Tania smiled warmly as her sleepy eyes took in the beautifully prepared breakfast. 'Very good,' she agreed. 'Did everyone else have breakfast in bed? It makes me feel very lazy.'

'*No, no, signorina*.' The plain face was shocked. 'But the *signore* say you tired. Is best. Then you come down.'

Tania nodded to show she had understood. 'Thank you, Candice, but call me Tania, won't you?'

'*No, no*.' If the maid's face had shown shock before it registered something akin to panic now as she backed hastily towards the half-open door. 'Is not right, *signorina*; I sorry.'

She was gone before Tania could call her back to explain, and she looked down ruefully at the tray on her lap. That was clearly her first mistake. How many more would she make before the end of the day?

After finishing her breakfast she carefully placed the tray on the floor and padded across to the window, opening the latticed wood shutters and flinging the diamond-leaded windows open wide so the cool bright air shivered on to her skin.

'Oh, how beautiful.' She breathed the words out loud into the glorious silence that surrounded her. The house overlooked wooded hills and deep valleys and was set in splendid isolation in its own extensive grounds within the huge stone wall that surrounded the perimeter of the property. Far in the distance in one of the meadows she could see a flock of sheep being herded along by a small swathed figure, the sound of the tiny bells they wore in necklaces sweet on the cold air.

She stood drinking in the tranquillity and peace of this magical vista for long enchanted moments before the chill of the soft air drove her from the window, and after a warm shower in her large ornate bathroom she dressed quickly in jeans and a warm jumper, brushing her hair into a shining pony-tail, high on her head.

'Nana!' Emmanuele's rapturous welcome was wonderfully normal as she entered the children's suite on the top floor of the west wing of the house. It had taken her five minutes to find their rooms, and initial apprehension at the sumptuous luxury surrounding her had slowly changed into barely concealed alarm as she had wandered down first one beautifully decorated passageway and then into other almost identical ones. She had been too mesmerised the evening before when Enrico had taken her to the children's room before dinner to notice their route—the lavish furnishings and sheer grand scale of the beautiful old mansion had temporarily robbed her of her wits.

'Tania?' Gilda looked surprised as she came out of Louisa's bathroom, carrying a stack of fluffy towels. 'What you doing here? The *signore* say he goin' to show you round. You see him?'

'No.' Tania looked sheepishly at the Italian woman. 'Candice did say I had to go downstairs but I wanted to see you all first.'

'*Sì.*' Gilda nodded understandingly. 'Is big place, eh? The *signore*, he like nice things, and his *madre*, his mother, she is, how you say,' she rolled her eyes expressively, 'the lizard?'

'Lizard?' Tania looked blank for a moment, and then she smiled slowly. 'I think you mean dragon, Gilda.'

'*Sì.*'

As she came down the stairs a few minutes later she saw Enrico was waiting for her, his head hidden behind a newspaper. He was seated in one of the highly embroidered chaise-longues dotting the vast hall, his head lifting instantly as he heard her light footsteps.

'Ah, Tania. Good morning. I trust you slept well?'

She looked at him as he got to his feet at her approach, tall, dark and unsmiling, with that strange expression shadowing the harsh planes of his face. 'Yes, thank you.' She was nervous and it showed in the tremor in her voice.

'Good.' His black eyes glittered as they swept over her flushed face. 'You look refreshed.'

'Gilda said you wanted to see me.'

'*Sì.* That is correct.' He suddenly seemed almost a stranger, the dark, powerful master of this small kingdom, where she had no doubt his word was law. 'I thought it would be best to show you the gardens and surrounding countryside before the rest of my guests arrive on Wednesday.

She stared at him wide-eyed. In England he had virtually held her at arm's length for those few miserable days before they had left, but now there was a subtle change in his manner that she couldn't quite put her finger on. Almost a possessive attitude that was not in keeping with what had gone before. It must be because he was annoyed at his mother's coolness and was determined to make her stay enjoyable. 'Thank you, I'd love that.' She smiled as she spoke and his eyes narrowed into black slits, flickering over her parted lips.

'It is settled, then. I will arrange for one of the cars to be brought round. There is fresh coffee in the breakfast-room if you would care for a cup before we leave?'

'Thank you.'

He opened a door to the right of him and gestured for her to enter before disappearing through a high arched opening at the end of the hall. She entered the room slowly, her thoughts churning. He hadn't smiled once through the whole exchange; it was almost as if he was on edge about something, but she was probably the last person he would confide a problem in. Even this proposed excursion was motivated by pity.

'*Ciao, Tania.*' Camillo's handsome face was warm with undisguised admiration and approval as she raised startled eyes at the sound of his voice. He was sitting finishing what had obviously been a huge breakfast, and she looked with laughing eyes at the array of plates scattered round his place at the big wooden table.

'I can see you like a good breakfast.'

He smiled cheerfully back at her, quite unabashed. 'I'm a big boy, or hadn't you noticed?' The teasing words carried a note of wry questioning that she chose to ignore.

'I'd noticed.' She poured herself a cup of coffee as she spoke, wondering how she could feel so relaxed and in charge of the situation with this man, whereas Enrico reduced her to a trembling wreck with one glance from his black eyes.

'I like the way you handled my aunt last night. I've been waiting to see someone do that for years. I've discovered quite a bit about you since then.'

'Really?' She raised curious eyebrows. 'Had a heart-to-heart with Enrico?' Her voice had a coolness that made his face straighten slightly.

'No way—you must be joking! No one asks my cousin for information, as I'm sure you must be aware. No, Gilda was very helpful after I'd bribed her by promising to take Emmanuele and Louisa out for the afternoon.'

'Oh.' She sipped the hot coffee, and he patted the empty seat by his side.

'Come on, sit down for a minute.' She settled herself in a chair a few yards from the one he had indicated, and he grimaced in laughing disapproval, his blue eyes bright and warm. 'I hear Enrico is showing you the sights of our wonderful country, then? Pity. I offered at breakfast to be your escort for the next few days, but he said you'd already promised him. You'd have had much more fun with me, you know.' It was said totally without rancour.

'Would I?' She answered automatically as she thought about his words. Why had Enrico said he had already asked her?

'You sure would. I'm amazed my venerable cousin can bear to take a few days off. He eats, sleeps and drinks work. The man is addicted to it.'

'Perhaps he doesn't have much else, besides the children, of course,' she added hastily as his thick eyebrows danced.

'Perhaps.' His voice was wry. 'It's not for the lack of opportunity, though. It's been like a fashion parade up here since Catalina died. Some of these women have no shame.'

Her heart gave a searing jolt but she kept her face bland and her voice calm. 'Are you part of the family empire?' Her voice was slightly caustic, and his eyes narrowed slightly.

'Do I detect a note of disapproval?' He smiled as she flushed a warm pink. 'Yes, I'm part of it. A somewhat minor part, I have to admit. I just don't seem to have the dedication that the worthy Enrico pours into it all. I find other... pursuits more interesting.'

His eyes were gleaming wickedly, and in spite of trying to keep a straight face she laughed softly. 'I don't doubt that for a minute.'

'Now don't jump to conclusions.' His voice assumed a note of mocking censure. 'I'm frequently misunderstood, you know. Just because I enjoy the company of the female sex and like to spend money rather than make it, I'm considered something of a dissolute in family circles.'

'How unfair.' She entered into the light-hearted banter gratefully. It was so good to laugh and joke with someone without any undercurrents.

'I can understand that talking to Tania is far more interesting than working, Camillo, but didn't I hear you say last night that there is a meeting to discuss the purchase of more vineyards at eleven? You have exactly an hour to get there, so I suggest you leave now.'

The cold voice from the doorway wiped the smile off Tania's face, and Camillo flashed her a rueful grimace as he rose from his seat. 'Sorry, Rico, my fault. I'll make it in time.'

'I hope so.' Enrico's voice was razor-sharp as he stared intently at his cousin. 'We've got a lot hanging on this deal and you promised me you were up to it.'

'I am, I am.' Camillo seemed remarkedly unoffended by his cousin's coldness, and his relaxed smiling face was in stark contrast to Enrico's black frown.

'See you later, Tania.' He left the room, walking with a lazy sensual prowl that seemed indicative of his nature, and Enrico was still frowning as he sat down in the seat his cousin had vacated.

'Don't encourage him.' His voice was low and controlled as he held her eyes with a cool stare. 'He's a good man at heart but the original wolf where women are concerned.'

'I beg your pardon?' Her blue eyes flashed with indignation. 'I did not encourage him.'

'No?' His voice was coldly disbelieving as he poured himself a cup of coffee and slowly added cream. 'Well, just don't. He should have taken over several functions of the business by now, but he's far too interested in playing about.'

'He was telling me.' She looked at him defiantly from under her lashes.

'Oh, I don't doubt it. That's the trouble with Camillo, he's just too amiable for his—and the business's—good. His social life is of prime importance and he doesn't mind admitting it. The man will drive me mad before he's finished.'

He ran a hand through his crisp black hair and she noticed he was looking tired. 'This estate is too much for one man to handle. I need someone I can trust at the helm, and he's only a few years younger than me, for crying out loud. I've waited long enough for him to settle down.'

'Tell him, then.' She shifted uneasily in her seat as his eyes gleamed coldly. 'Stop carrying him and he'll have to sink or swim. Surely he's enough of a Meliora to swim?'

'Oh, you've deduced that after a couple of meetings? That's very astute of you.' His voice had a flint-like quality that cut through the air. 'I let him have a free rein, then?'

'If you like.'

'I don't like, as it happens. You are seriously telling me I should put my cousin in charge of very important projects and just sit back and wait for the results? Do you realise he could lose hundreds of thousands of pounds with one ill-timed decision?'

'You can afford it, can't you?' She looked at him as an expression of sheer incredulity ran over the harsh features. 'I'm sure you made the odd mistake at first. If he did make a blunder you can be sure he wouldn't do it again. Sometimes the only way to learn is by your mistakes.'

'You're very generous with my money.'

'Oh, money!' She waved her hand irritably at him. 'For someone who has so much of it, it seems to dominate your life. You don't trust any women because you think they love your wealth and not you, you blame Camillo for wanting to enjoy life a little and not take everything so seriously. Money isn't the be-all and end-all——'

'That's enough!' His voice was savage and as she raised her eyes to his again she saw a deep cold rage in his dark eyes. 'Who are you to tell me I'm handling my life all wrong? I would have thought you had learnt your lesson after your last effort at reading my mind. When will you learn to keep quiet? I'm sure Camillo would be extremely appreciative to hear you defending him with such intensity, but it is not necessary. As I'm sure you have noticed, he is a grown man and quite able to take care of himself.'

Her blue eyes opened wide with amazement. There had been a vicious innuendo in those last words, and his lips were curled back in disgust.

'Now just hang on a minute.' Her voice shook, but hot rage turned her cheeks fiery red. 'If you think that I'm trying to... that I want...'

'What is it you are trying to say?' Mocking cynicism coloured the dark voice. 'Have I accused you of anything?'

'No, but——'

'Then let the matter rest.' She looked at him in bewildered silence. If the idea hadn't been so impossible she would almost have thought he was jealous of the interest Camillo had shown in her, but that was laughable.

'Did Camillo tell you he has offered to take you sightseeing?' The cold face was shuttered and still, and as she nodded miserably he rose and walked to the large picture-window, standing with his back to her. 'The idea was quite out of the question; his work-load is too large at the moment. However, I had arranged to spend some time with my family, so my services in that direction are available. You understand?'

She nodded again at his uninterested back. So the tour had been Camillo's idea, after all; Enrico had been forced into escorting her. 'If he offers again you will refuse politely. I don't want him wasting time before the Christmas break.'

He swung round as he spoke and glanced at her pale face. 'Come on, it's not so bad, is it?' There was a watchfulness in his eyes she didn't understand.

'No, of course not.' She lowered her head. 'But there is no need for anyone to take me anywhere. I'm quite happy here with the children and Gilda.'

'Nevertheless, it is arranged. Please get your coat and we will leave.'

The rest of the day was bitter-sweet. Enrico was the perfect companion, informative host and gently courteous consort, while being very careful to keep their conversation friendly and bland. His nearness was a subtle torment to Tania, and she was almost glad to get back to the house as dusk fell, after a day of feasting on gorgeous tranquil countryside full of rolling hillsides and copses. She had never realised Italy was a country of such vast contrasts, white sandy beaches and azure seas combining wonderfully with rich artistic heritage.

They had eaten at midday at a tiny rural tavern where a huge log fire had banished the chill from the air, dining like kings on a mouth-watering pizza, the likes of which Tania had never tasted before, topped with a delicious pale gorgonzola cheese that tasted wonderful. The wine had been dry and sparkling, in perfect harmony with the meal, and Tania had eaten until she had thought she would burst.

'Full?' Enrico's eyes were quietly smiling as she finished the meal, with a tender indulgent gleam that vanished instantly as he caught her gaze.

'That was wonderful,' she answered gratefully, nibbling at a succulent fig from the large bowl in the middle of the small wooden table, and licking her fingers in unconscious approval. He followed her tongue as it slid over her sticky fingers, a sudden dark heat in his eyes that caused her breath to catch in her throat.

'Time to go.' His words were wooden, and she shook herself mentally as she rose from the table, waiting for him at the open door while he talked to the innkeeper and his wife. She must stop imagining that these glances of his meant anything. He had made it perfectly clear that he found her feelings for him a total embarrassment.

The next two days sped by, and before she realised it it was Christmas Eve. Emmanuele and Louisa were wild with excitement, their exuberance bringing many a sharp rebuke from their grandmother. Enrico's mother had graciously asked Tania to call her by her first name, Lucia, but Tania felt quite unable to be so familiar with the tall, proud, aristocratic woman she now respected but still disliked. She ruled the family with authoritative coldness, bowing only to Enrico's will as master of the house, and her attitude to Tania had not mellowed in the slightest. The hard brown eyes followed her in icy disapproval whenever they were in the same room, and Tania had taken to spending most of her time in the children's quarters, where she kept Gilda company.

Overnight the servants had decorated the ground floor with festive adornment, and a huge fir tree stood in the hall, its branches covered with hundreds of tiny candles and stars, and a myriad gaily wrapped packages underneath its spreading green branches. Tania and the children stood transfixed at their first sight of it, and Enrico laughed softly from his vantage-point as he came out of the breakfast-room.

'I don't know whose mouth is wider,' he said lazily, his dark eyes soft and warm on her glowing face. 'Haven't you ever seen a Christmas tree before?'

'Not like this,' she breathed quietly. 'It's gorgeous.'

'For now, but its beauty will soon fade.'

'Don't.' Her voice was high with disappointment. 'Don't spoil it.'

He looked at her distressed face, the retort he had been about to make dying on his lips, and slowly moved to join her at the bottom of the stairs, his eyes suddenly gentle. 'Don't be so vulnerable.' His voice carried an undercurrent of pain in its rich depths. 'Haven't you learnt by now you have to cultivate a shell from the rest of the world?'

'I can't,' she said simply, looking up into his dark face with her heart glowing in her eyes, her love for him plain to read.

Time stood still for long silent seconds as they drank from each other's eyes without speaking, a curious hunger in his face that turned the proud features into hard stone. 'It's no good, Tania.' He echoed the words he had said that night in the midst of the English countryside with the snow forming a soft white blanket protecting them from prying eyes. 'I would destroy you the way I destroyed her.'

She stared at him, seeing nothing but the agonising heartache in his eyes. 'That wouldn't matter.' Her words were a whisper. 'I'd take that chance.'

He flinched from her as though she had horrified him. 'Well, I wouldn't.' He disappeared through the archway at the end of the hall with firm measured steps, his face closed and cold, leaving her trembling and shaken as the children touched the tree with inquisitive fingers.

How was she going to get through this Christmas until she could go home and lick her wounds in peace? Didn't he have any idea of what he was doing to her?

CHAPTER NINE

IT WAS easier when all the unexpected relatives arrived later that morning. In the hustle and bustle no one noticed Tania's white face and by midday she had recovered her equilibrium sufficiently to appear normal.

After a buffet lunch most of the guests settled down quietly to chat and read, a few retiring to their rooms for an afternoon nap. Tania tried to interest herself in a book she had brought from England, but after the words kept jumping round in circles and she had read the same paragraph three times still without understanding a word she decided to go for a walk in the grounds.

Emmanuele and Louisa were fast asleep, with the ever-vigilant Gilda quietly knitting outside their rooms, so after collecting her coat and slipping her feet into small fluffy boots she quietly made her way downstairs and out on to the large sweeping steps at the front of the house.

'And where might you be creeping off to?' Enrico's voice was teasing but it still caused her to jump as he came up behind her. She hadn't noticed that he had seen her leaving.

'I'm just going for a walk.' She looked up at him shyly. 'That is all right, isn't it? Gilda is with the children and—— '

'Good grief, Tania.' His voice was sharp. 'You don't have to justify your movements to me. Of course it's all right.' She bit her lip; he always seemed so angry lately.

His expression softened as he caught the look on her face. 'Would you care for some company, or would you prefer to be alone?'

'I'd love you to come,' she answered simply, keeping her voice bland with some effort. He smiled warmly.

'Let me get my jacket and we'll be off.'

They had been walking for some minutes when Enrico broke the silence, the content of his words bringing her eyes up to his face in sharp surprise. 'I'm sorry for my mother's behaviour towards you, Tania.' He was clearly embarrassed. 'All I can say is that her stance holds no personal animosity.'

'It doesn't?' Tania tried to keep the note of disbelief out of her voice, but failed.

'No, not really. I don't know how to explain it.' He glanced at her enquiring face and then away again, keeping his eyes straight in front as they walked along a smooth, well-kept path into a big tiered area full of small fountains and tiny pools in which brightly coloured fish were darting here and there in the cool sunshine.

'She belongs to the old school, I suppose. In her day social strata were very clearly defined. Thankfully we are now drawing away from such an archaic attitude, but she won't move with the times.'

'I see.' Tania's cheeks burnt with colour and his own face was slightly red.

'I just didn't want you to think she didn't like you as a person. She really rather admires you, I think.'

'It's not important.' She glanced up at him walking by her side. He must have trod these grounds with Catalina many a time. She would have had the right to slip her arm in his and lean against him as they walked. They had probably kissed in this very place—— She forced her thoughts away from the path they were taking.

It was no use torturing herself. She must just make the most of these next few days and not think beyond that.

'You're very quiet.' He looked down at her consideringly.

'Does that mean you think I usually talk too much?' She made her voice teasing but he didn't respond to the sally.

'No, I don't think you talk too much, Tania.' His voice was rich and deep, and as she glanced up at him she was caught and held by the dark fire in his eyes.

'You don't?' She was whispering without knowing why. He shook his head as his body turned, and he pulled her into his arms. His movement had been so violent that for a moment she was crushed against his hard frame with her hands imprisoned against his chest.

He nuzzled the top of her head. 'Your hair is so soft, like silk. It shimmers in the sun with so many lights that it looks alive.' His voice was gruff, and one hand raised her chin so that she was forced to look up into his dark face. 'I've been wanting to do this for days.' As his lips fastened on hers they held a fierce hunger that was stronger than ever before. The intensity of it frightened her, and for a moment she stiffened in his embrace before the heat of his passion kindled her own desire and she relaxed against him with a little moan.

As he felt her yield to his body he growled low in his throat; his tongue searched the sweetness of her mouth and she gladly allowed him to penetrate its inner depths. His hand curved into her waist, moulding her against him so closely that she could scarcely breathe. 'I want you, Tania; you've got under my skin...' His mouth searched the hollows beneath her ears, her closed eyelids, her throat as his breath shuddered against her flesh. His lips were doing indescribable things to her senses, her heart was hammering against her ribs and she could feel a slow sweet throb in her lower stomach that had her pressing against him for relief.

His hands slid down the length of her body beneath her coat and she pushed aside the thick tweed of his jacket, feeling the bunched muscles in his chest and shoulders under the thin silk of his shirt as her hands moved hungrily over the hard planes of his body. 'Oh, yes, touch me, Tania; you're driving me mad...' His voice was a hoarse groan and he found her mouth again, bending down to reach her so that his big body seemed to encompass all around her and there was nothing real in the world except him.

'I need you, Tania, I need you more than I've ever...' His voice trailed away as his hands became still. There had been something in his words that had blocked the fierce hunger that was devouring him, staunching its flow as effectively as a cold shower, as though his own need had shocked him.

A cold sensation trickled over her skin as she raised her eyes to his face. He was looking at her as though he had never seen her before, an expression of such cold withdrawal on his face that she almost cried out against it.

'What's the matter?' Her voice was a tiny whisper and he stared at her uncomprehendingly, pushing her away slightly, his hands falling to his sides as he took a step backwards, moving from her as though she were poison.

'I'm sorry, Tania. That was unforgivable.' His voice was full of self-contempt and she looked at him bewilderedly as he turned away. 'It's getting cold. We'd better return to the house—the party will start soon.'

She buttoned her coat with hands that shook, following behind him almost at a run as he strode back

towards the house with savage strides. He opened the
door for her and immediately disappeared into his study,
shutting the door with a firm click and leaving her
standing in the hall, feeling more alone than she had
ever felt in all her life.

She spent the rest of the afternoon in her room, sitting
in numb misery, staring out at the beautiful rolling
countryside until it was time to get ready for the festivities planned for that night.

A long hot bath soaked away some of the stiffness
that was cramping her limbs, and after washing her hair
and brushing it dry until it shone like molten copper she
applied a little light make-up carefully, adding a spot of
colour to her pale cheeks and darkening her eyelids to
disguise the pale mauve shadows beneath. She looped
her hair into a high loose knot on the top of her head,
allowing a few curling tendrils to soften the pure line of
her neck and fall over her brow.

She was just going to leave her room when there was
a soft knock on the door, and, expecting to see Gilda
with the children, she opened the door with a quick
flourish.

'Oh!' For the life of her she couldn't think of a word
to say as she took in Enrico, standing in the shadowed
hallway, his big body leaning against the far wall.

'Are you ready?' His eyes were wretched as they looked
at her slim body in the dim light, his face a grim dark
mask in the half-light.

'Yes, I'm ready.' She looked at him, noting the tiny
white lines prominent around the firm mouth, and the
exhaustion grooving its path round his eyes. In spite of
her own hurt and pain, she suddenly longed to help him.
He was obviously going through some torment she knew
nothing about.

'Don't worry about this afternoon, Enrico.' She spoke quickly before she lost her nerve. 'It's all forgotten.'

He made a small exclamation deep in his throat as he looked at her concerned face. 'I'm a very selfish man, Tania. I wanted you to come with me and spend Christmas in my home because I needed you here, even knowing it would hurt both of us. Can you understand that?'

She shook her head gently. 'Not really, if I'm honest.'

'It's probably just as well.'

He said no more as they walked down the huge winding staircase to find the party in full swing, the sound of laughter making the high ceiling ring. It was like no party she had ever been to in England—there was so much hilarity and fun, with impromptu dancing that excluded no one and a general feeling of such warmth and gaiety that she found before long that she was actually enjoying herself.

Hot punch was served just before midnight and then, to her astonishment, the whole assembly trooped to the tiny chapel built some way from the main house in the grounds, where hundreds of candles had been lit, 'To welcome the Christ child,' Camillo whispered in her ear.

After prayers and a Bible reading by Enrico, they each lit a long white candle and placed it round the small home-made crib at the front of the small altar. 'You must say a prayer when it's your turn,' Camillo whispered again, and she nodded gratefully, glad to have a friendly face beside her in this strange environment.

As she left her seat to walk the few feet to the front of the tiny church she noticed Enrico's dark head bowed in prayer, his lips twisted as though in pain. She lit the candle carefully and closed her eyes as the full beauty of Christmas swept over her, a deep peace settling on her bruised mind. 'Help me to help him,' she prayed silently, 'that's all I ask.' She left the chapel, convinced that a higher authority had taken the burden on to His shoulders.

They sang carols back in the main house until the early hours, when Enrico called a halt to the festivities. He had not joined in the last part of the evening, standing to one side of the merry throng, his face harsh and withdrawn as he had smoked one small cheroot after another.

Christmas Day began with the children tearing into her room with their favourite presents, their small faces flushed with excitement. They snuggled down into the large bed either side of her, their warm little bodies bringing immeasurable comfort to her bruised spirit. She read them a story from Louisa's new fairy-tale book, and it was like this that Enrico found them when he came searching for his offspring an hour or so later.

'I might have known they'd be here,' he said smilingly from the doorway, his face tender as he looked at the three of them burrowed deep into the covers. Tania met his gaze over the children's heads, and something jerked deep in her chest with a sharp throb of pain. If only...

It was lunchtime two days later when the shrill ringing of the telephone interrupted their midday meal. Most of the guests had gone home earlier that morning, and there were only the two original aunts and Camillo, besides Enrico's immediate family.

Enrico came back to the table with a worried frown wrinkling his brow. 'We're going to have to pay a visit to the new wine-presses, Camillo.' He held up his hand as Camillo went to protest. 'I know, I know, we're on holiday till next week, but this latest deal is going sour on us and we've got to sort it out quickly.' He turned to his mother apologetically. 'You understand, *Mamma*?'

His mother nodded her head in resigned acceptance. 'Go! Go!' Lucia flapped her hands as though she were shooing away a pair of chickens. 'We'll wait dinner for you.'

It was long after the normal mealtime when Enrico and Camillo returned. Enrico ate his food in morose silence, and the atmosphere at the dinner table was sombre.

'I'm going to have to fly to Cantante to sort out the legal side.' Enrico pushed his half-full plate away from him as he looked at Camillo. 'Can you take care of things here?'

'Of course.' Camillo seemed supremely untroubled by it all. 'You worry too much, Rico.'

'It's just as well someone in this family does!' The retort was sharp and stinging, and for once Camillo flushed a deep scarlet as he stared across at his cousin over the table. 'When are you going to wake up to the fact we could lose the contract if we don't deliver on time? That piece of paper you signed tied us up in knots.'

'I got the legal brains to go over it as you suggested.' Camillo's voice was sulky. 'Is it my fault if they screwed up?'

'No, you're right.' Enrico relaxed back in his chair with a deep sigh and ran his hand over his face in tired exasperation. 'I apologise, Camillo.'

Camillo shrugged easily, but Tania noticed the smile on his lips didn't meet his eyes, which had suddenly became a deep icy blue. He had clearly resented his cousin's accusation that he was to blame.

They were just finishing coffee when Enrico stood up slowly, reaching across and touching Tania on the shoulder. 'Come into my study for a moment, would you, Tania? I'm not sure how long I shall be away and

there are some matters I would like you to attend to if
I'm gone for long.'

She followed him into the large book-lined room in
silence, more than a little perturbed at the way events
had moved. She didn't like the thought of being in a
foreign country with Enrico gone. She realised with a
little pang that, morose and difficult as he was at times,
the big dark man now slumped at the shiny desk in front
of her was of immense comfort in a strange environment.

'What do you want me to do?' She stared at him over
the papers scattered on the smooth wood.

'Kiss me.' The retort was so unexpected that she gazed
at him with her mouth half open and her eyes wide.

'What?'

'Kiss me.' A slight smile crinkled the corners of his
eyes suddenly as he took in her amazed expression. 'You
asked me what I wanted you to do, so I told you.'

She looked at him warily. There was that mocking,
teasing note in his voice and his face was unreadable.
She had no idea whether he was serious or not, so she
said and did nothing, her face flushing a dull pink

'Come here.' He held out his hand and she moved
forward slowly, her eyes apprehensive. What game was
he playing now?

She stopped in front of him and he pulled her down
on to his lap with a small sigh. 'I'm sorry, Tania, I'm
probably being most unfair, but today has been one hell
of a time and I need a bit of human comfort.' He nuzzled
her head again the way he had in the garden, turning
her round so she was leaning back against him, resting
against his hard chest.

'You're like a drug; do you know that?' The deep voice
in her ear was dry with self-mockery. 'Every time I think

I've kicked the habit I find myself in need of another fix. I don't like it, but I don't seem able to master it.'

'Oh.' There was nothing else she could say.

He turned her round quickly and kissed her lips fleetingly before lifting her up and depositing her in the chair facing the desk. 'Don't look so frightened. I wasn't going to eat you.' It wasn't fright that had widened her eyes, and the thought of being eaten by him was exquisite, but she shook her head gently as she looked down at her hands.

'I know. You surprised me, that's all.'

'I took your advice with regard to my cousin, by the way.'

'You did?' She was astonished and it showed. 'Why, what have you done?'

'I've decided it's ridiculous for me to half kill myself trying to be everything to everybody. I had been running the whole caboodle for five years at his age, so it won't hurt him to take a little more responsibility for some of the Italian side of the business. I can deal with matters abroad and still have time to be...' he paused and his eyes were glittering and dark on her face '...less of a dried-up shell.'

'That's good,' she said quietly.

'Emmanuele and Louisa are growing fast and they need to see more of me. Do you agree?'

'Of course.' She looked at him searchingly, noting the strange look in his eyes. 'That will be nice for them.'

'Nice.' His mouth lingered on the word. 'Yes, it will be nice.' It was as though he wanted to say something more but restrained from doing so.

'So, Camillo will be around if anything should go wrong while I'm away. He has a list of my movements and you can contact me any time.'

'I'm sure nothing will go wrong.'

'I hope not.' He stood up suddenly and came to sit on the desk in front of her. 'The hell of it is I don't want to go, Tania, and do you know why?'

'No.' The whole conversation was becoming too much for her. Her head was beginning to ache with the tension in the air.

'I'd like to be here with the children and ... you.' The last word had seemed forced out of him, and for a second a deep throb of joy pierced her before she noticed the haunted expression on his face. 'That's crazy, isn't it?'

'I don't think it's crazy.'

'Ah, but you don't know what goes on in here, do you?' He tapped the side of his head slowly. 'You'd run screaming if you did.' His jaw was tense as though some inner conflict was causing intense physical pain.

'I don't think I would ever run from you.' Her words were very soft and she knew even as she spoke that they were probably a grave mistake. They stared at each other for a full minute, and then he shook his head slowly.

'What am I doing? I must be mad.' He leant forward and gently, very gently, placed his mouth on hers. The kiss was undemanding and incredibly sweet, and for a moment there was such a drumming in her ears that she felt as though she would faint. It seemed a promise of things to come and yet she dared not let herself hope for more. A further rejection would be too agonising to bear.

'I'll see you before I leave in the morning.' He had stood up and moved to the door, his face more tender than she had ever seen it before.

'All right.' She walked in dazed submission past him and went up to her room quietly. There was no way she could make polite conversation with the others that evening. Her head was pounding with words and all she wanted to do was lie in the scented darkness until sleep claimed her senses. She had never felt so mixed up in all her life.

At breakfast the next morning Tania began to wonder if the episode in the study had been a figment of her imagination. Enrico was his usual austere self, his black eyes hooded and cold and his face harshly handsome and expressionless. She glanced at him once or twice as they ate, but his gaze seemed to pass right through her and there was no flicker of warmth in it.

After breakfast he disappeared into the study with Camillo for some time, and Tania wandered upstairs to join Gilda and the children. So much for dreams...

It was just ten o'clock when they heard his unmistakable footsteps outside the children's suite of rooms, and Tania's heart did a quick somersault. Stop it, she said silently to herself as the children ran squealing to the tall dark figure in the doorway. He's come to say goodbye to Emmanuele and Louisa, not you. She made herself tidy some books and toys as he squatted down and took the children into his arms, warning them to behave and be good while he was gone.

'Haven't you got a kind word for the weary warrior before he goes off to do battle?' He was standing before her and they were alone. Gilda must have taken the children downstairs.

'I hope it all goes well for you,' she said stiffly as she looked into his smiling face, her eyes shadowed with uncertainty. He was such an enigma, this big silent man with his fiery nature and cold thoughts.

'I wanted to say goodbye to you properly.' He was so close that she could smell the fresh clean scent of him, and her stomach muscles bunched tightly.

'I thought you'd forgotten.' He looked puzzled as she spoke and she flicked her head towards the door, causing her hair to brush her face in a red cloud. 'You seemed so preoccupied downstairs.'

His eyes never left her face and his voice was low and deep as he replied. 'I could tell you every morsel that passed your lips at breakfast. It's the first time in my life I've envied a piece of toast.' There was a throb of amusement in the last sentence and she laughed softly at the wry look on his face. 'I'm just not very good at wearing my heart on my sleeve.'

'I don't understand.' She looked up into his eyes and he shook his head slightly.

'I think you are probably the only woman of my acquaintance who could say that and mean it.' He drew her into his arms roughly. 'I'm not an easy man to be around, Tania. It would have been better for you if you had never met me.'

'Maybe.' Her heart was in her eyes.

'I want you more than I have ever wanted any woman in my life.'

'Just want?' The words were forced past her lips of their own volition.

His hands moved up and down her arms restlessly and his face was troubled. 'It's the best I can do. Maybe you were right, after all—a dried-up shell. I don't know.' He raised her chin in that gesture she was beginning to know and brushed her mouth with his firm cool lips. 'I'll see you in a few days.' He let her go abruptly and walked to the door, only to turn with his hand on the knob and move across the room in two strides.

'Come here.' This time he moulded her slender frame into his until she could feel every hard contour of his body, and his mouth was hot and searching on hers. His touch triggered an uncontrollable response, and as he felt her begin to tremble in his arms his breathing grew ragged and harsh. 'You're driving me insane...' It was almost as though he wanted to crush her into his very soul as the kiss became almost a punishment in its intensity. He was bruising her lips with the force of his passion but she welcomed the pain. If this strange animal desire was the most he could feel for her she would take that for now and be grateful; later he might learn to love her. He had to—the force of her love alone would make him. It all seemed so very simple when he was holding her close like this, totally hers for a few brief moments.

'Goodbye, Tania.' He had gone before she could even say his name, leaving her swaying and shaken in the middle of the room, her hand going to her lips, which still bore his brand.

She felt as though she was living in an odd sort of limbo over the next few days. The time came and went for them to return to England, but Enrico sent a message through Camillo to tell them to wait until he returned to Casa delle Querce so that he could escort them home personally. There was little for her to do in the day; Gilda took care of the children and, apart from the few hours she spent with them, time hung heavy on her hands. She found herself looking forward to the time Camillo returned home in the evening—his, at least, was a friendly face and he took it upon himself to entertain her, proving to be an amusing and witty companion. He offered to take her out for the evening on several occasions, but she always refused; she had a feeling Enrico would not approve of his cousin's escorting her anywhere if it meant the two of them would be alone. He accepted her decision in the way he did everything, with a smile, a shrug and a slight Latin tilt to his dark blond head. There was never any tension with Camillo; he was most comfortable to be around.

It was the evening of the fifth day since Enrico had left, and Lucia had been particularly testy all day, retiring mid-afternoon to her rooms with a migraine. There were just the two aunts, Camillo and Tania at the dinner table, and for once Tania found herself enjoying the meal. Usually Lucia's frosty disposition cast a sombre cloud over the proceedings, but even the two aunts seemed almost jovial as they listened to Camillo's banter with indulgent smiles.

'Drink up, Tania, we've got something to celebrate tonight.' His sparkling blue eyes were laughing at her as he refilled her half-empty glass and those of the aunts, causing them to squeal in protest and put their wrinkled hands over the rims in twittering disapproval.

'Why, what's happened?' She smiled back at him as she spoke; it was so easy to enter into his merry mood. She vaguely realised he must have poured her three glasses of wine during the meal and this was the fourth. She really mustn't have any more.

'Enrico has cleared the difficulties at his end and the deal is on again.' He was looking directly at her now and his gaze seemed to hold her eyes transfixed with its intensity. 'That means the big man will be all smiles again.' Just for a moment she felt there was some bitterness in his voice, but then he gave that charmingly boyish smile that told her she must be mistaken.

'That's good.' She found she was having to concentrate very hard so that her words were clear, and her lips felt strangely dry. She ran her tongue over them, missing the heat that narrowed Camillo's gaze as he noticed the gesture.

The two old aunts struggled to their feet and made their farewells as they finished dinner, their progress to the stairs a little erratic. 'I do believe you've made them tipsy.' Tania looked laughingly at the two small black-clad figures giggling softly as they weaved towards their rooms.

'I have?' His face was wickedly innocent as he leaned back in his chair. 'Quite unintentional, I assure you.'

'Enrico wouldn't like it.'

He nodded in agreement. 'No, I don't suppose he would, but then, he doesn't like a lot of things, does he?' He picked up his wine glass as he spoke and stood up slowly, reaching across for hers. 'Come and sit down in the drawing-room for a while. It was a bit nippy earlier on and I asked Candice to light the fire. It should still be quite warm.'

'I think I'll go straight up to my room, if you don't mind, Camillo.' She stifled a yawn with difficulty. 'I think I've had a little too much wine and it's getting late.'

'Oh, come on, Tania.' His deep voice was gently pleading as he took her arm. 'Enrico will come back soon and that means you'll be leaving us. I've enjoyed the last few evenings immensely, and I feel we're just getting to know each other. Just a few minutes.' She looked into his open friendly face and nodded slowly.

'OK, just a few minutes, then.'

He refilled both their glasses before they left the room, despite her protest, and, carrying them carefully, he led the way to the silent drawing-room, where a huge log fire was burning brightly in the polished hearth. She noticed someone had pulled a settee close to the warmth and that there was just one lamp burning in the corner of the room, and felt a moment's apprehension. It all looked a little too cosy. She hesitated just inside the door, wondering how she could go to her room without causing offence.

'I must sort through some papers in a while before I go up,' Camillo said cheerfully, placing their glasses on a small wooden table to one side of the settee and patting the space invitingly next to him as he sat down with a small sigh. 'It's been a hell of a week, with one thing and another. I shall be glad when Enrico comes home.'

The casual conversational tone of his voice reassured her, and it seemed churlish not to join him. She sat down beside him carefully, with her back straight, and if he noticed her stiffness he didn't comment, simply passing her her glass with a light smile and beginning to talk easily about the day's events.

After a few minutes she found herself relaxing as the warmth from the glowing wood, combined with the mellow wine, made her eyelids ridiculously heavy. Camillo's voice was soothing and he didn't require any answers; she felt her tired limbs sinking into the soft velvet and a drowsy sluggishness taking over her senses.

'You're very beautiful, Tania.' He had been silent for some time and she was just falling asleep when the soft voice whispered close to her ear. 'I suppose you know how I feel about you?' As her eyes snapped open and she struggled to sit upright she was aware of his body moving across hers so that she was imprisoned beneath his superior weight. 'Just one kiss, Tania; I won't hurt you.'

His mouth fell on to hers even as he spoke, and she was suddenly encompassed by his long, lean frame. The kiss wasn't unpleasant—more gently seductive, indicative of his undoubted experience with the opposite sex. When she twisted beneath his body he moved away instantly, his face softly questioning as she pushed him away. 'Don't, please don't.'

She lay cradled against him as he raised himself slightly to look deep into her flushed face. 'Is it Enrico?' His voice was resigned but not unkind, and as quick tears flooded into her eyes he nodded slowly. 'I might have guessed. He has all the luck.'

The door opening and the lights going on happened in the same instant and brought them jerking apart. Enrico stood in the doorway with a look of amazed incredulity slowly darkening his face as his glittering eyes swept across their guilty faces.

'I want an explanation.' He was talking directly to Camillo as though Tania were invisible. 'And this time, little cousin, it had better be a good one.' His voice was like a whiplash, and for the first time in her life Tania knew what it was to be literally frozen with fear.

CHAPTER TEN

CAMILLO was on his feet in an instant, his handsome face as white as a sheet. 'This isn't what you think, Rico.' His voice was gently placating, but Enrico shot him a glance of pure contempt.

'No? And what am I thinking?' His gaze moved to Tania, who had stumbled to her feet, her hair ruffled and her clothes dishevelled. 'Tidy yourself.' The scathing bitterness in his deep voice was like the searing crack of a whip on bare flesh, and she winced helplessly.

'We were just having a drink before going to bed.' As black eyebrows raised themselves in sardonic fury Camillo realised he had expressed himself incredibly badly in the circumstances. 'I mean to our separate beds, Tania to hers and I to mine...' He was floundering and cast panic-stricken eyes to Tania, but she was beyond speech. The icy coldness in those dark eyes had chilled her blood and numbed her brain.

'I thought better of you, Camillo.' Enrico seemed to have gained control of himself; his face had set into pure stone and his big body was rigid. 'I left Tania in your care as a guest in this house. You disappoint me. I thought you understood that your liaisons were to be conducted out of harm's way.'

'Rico——' Whatever further protest Camillo might have made was halted by one glance from the coal-black eyes.

'Leave us, Camillo.' It was not a request. 'I'll speak to you in the morning.'

'Let me explain——'

'You're pushing me too far, cousin. For sake of family unity, I suggest you leave the room—*now*!' The last word was bitten out through clenched teeth, and Camillo left without another word and without even glancing at Tania.

Enrico kicked the door shut without taking his eyes off Tania's white face, but moved no further into the room, his body taut and still and his eyes narrowed.

'You know you really had me believing that pure and innocent routine.' His voice was quiet and deadly. 'Not at first, not with your looks, but later . . . yes, later.' His face twisted. 'How many have there been, Tania? I can't believe you were giving Camillo what you haven't given other men before. Or maybe the prize wasn't high enough before? What did my cousin promise? That he would marry you?' He gave a bark of laughter that tore at her. 'Then the joke is on you.'

She couldn't believe he was speaking to her like this, and yet part of her wanted to reach out and touch him, draw him to her, stop this raging pain and fury that was turning his eyes into steel-cold blades. 'You must let me explain——'

'How can you explain away that?' He flicked his hand savagely at the couch. 'Don't insult my intelligence on top of everything else. The room was in virtual darkness and you were making love to my cousin. There is nothing more to be said.'

As he turned to go she leapt across the room without knowing what she was doing, just driven by a desperate compulsion to make him stop and listen to her. 'Listen to me, Enrico, please . . .'

'I'll arrange for you to leave first thing in the morning.' His voice was icy cold. 'You've caused me nothing but trouble since the first day I saw you. I shall be glad to be rid of you.'

'Oh, and what good fortune have you brought me?' His words had stung her to the quick, and white-hot rage was coursing through her veins. She wanted to fly at him, to bite and scratch and kick until he was helpless before her. She was standing facing him now, her eyes shooting blue sparks. 'You've taken over my life and forced me to do everything I didn't want to. I never even wanted the job in the first place. You blackmailed me into it.'

'I did what?' For a split-second amazement took over the anger on his face. 'You accepted my offer of your own free will. It was *you* who came to *me*, remember.'

'Only because I was sorry for you.' As his body tensed she knew she had touched him on the raw. 'When I saw you in the hospital and——'

'And the way you respond when I make love to you? Is that because you feel sorry for me?' His voice dripped sarcasm and she could only stare with haunted blue eyes into his harshly cynical face. 'Or maybe that was all an act too? Perhaps you were prepared to endure my disgusting attention in the hope of winning first prize?'

'First prize?' All anger had fled from her body and her voice was a tiny whisper.

'Don't pretend you didn't have your eyes set on the chance of becoming the next Mrs Meliora. I can see it all now—your apparent fondness for the children, the way you have ingratiated yourself into my life. Perhaps you were growing tired of waiting and thought Camillo would be easier bait?' She gave a small moan, but the granite-hard voice went on relentlessly. 'You're just like all the rest, aren't you? Maybe a little more devious, but no different under the skin.'

'I hate you.'

He could barely hear her, but his mouth moved in a cruel sneer as his lips drew back from his teeth. 'Good. At least you are being honest now. Hate is an emotion I can actually believe in.'

'And love?'

He gave a low growl deep in his throat. 'Love! There is no such thing for most people. A few are unfortunate enough to get entangled in its brutal grip, but they quickly learn the futility of such a weakness.'

'I pity you.' Her words were clear and stark, and he recoiled almost as though she had hit him. 'From the bottom of my heart I pity you.' She raised her head slightly and looked straight into the dark face she loved so dearly and would soon never see again. 'One day you are going to look back over your life and scream for it to be different, but it will be too late.' She brushed past him and opened the door, leaving him standing silent and alone in the quiet room.

It was raining when she stepped off the plane in England, and the day was grey and dark. The airport smelt of wet clothes and luggage and seemed full of crying children and harassed, irritable parents.

She forced her mind to stay in the numb stupor that had taken over her senses from the time she had awoken that morning as a little boy of Emmanuele's age and build ran past her, squealing noisily. She mustn't allow herself to think here, to feel; she wouldn't be able to stand it. She must wait until she got to Great Oaks and then decide what to do. Her mind seized gratefully on the task in hand as though it was beyond coping with more than one instruction at a time.

She hadn't seen Enrico since that terrible scene the
night before. He had already left for the office with
Camillo when she had ventured downstairs first thing
that morning, and she had immediately requested Gilda's
help in ringing the airport and reserving a seat on the
first available flight that day. It had been economy class,
but that suited her budget. She could just about pay for
the ticket and the taxi fare to Great Oaks and then she
was penniless if she was going to pay Enrico the second
half of his payment to Mrs Jenkins.

Daisy and May were all but waiting on the doorstep
when she reached Great Oaks, answering her tired knock
immediately and ushering her into the welcoming warmth
with hugs and kisses. She discovered that Gilda had tele-
phoned them to let them know of her arrival; the Italian
woman had been in floods of tears when she had left
that morning. She had told her a little of what had transpired the night before, enough to let her know that there
was no possibility of her continuing to be employed by
Enrico. Gilda had been distraught, communicating her
distress to the children, which had made the parting
doubly painful.

'I've got a nice hot meal all ready,' Daisy said cheerfully, casting a horrified glance at her sister as they took
in Tania's exhausted face and tired eyes. 'Come and eat
before you do anything else.'

'I couldn't, really.' Tania felt this show of kindness
was going to be the last straw; the flood of tears that
she had held dammed back all day was threatening to
break through. 'I've only come to collect my things.'

'You aren't going out again tonight, ducky.' Daisy cast
an eye to the window where a cold misty dusk was
sending the raindrops in huge swirls to batter against the
glass. 'It'll be dark soon.' She took Tania's arm and drew

her into the warm kitchen. 'Now you get something inside of you and then you can tell us all about it. A trouble shared is a trouble halved, I always say.' May was nodding furiously in agreement and they both had identical smiles of encouragement stretching their plump faces, which froze in dismay as Tania sank down on to a chair, and putting her head on the clean scrubbed table, began to cry as though her heart would break.

'Come on, lovey, nothing can be as bad as this.' The two sisters had been sitting either side of her for more than ten minutes, patting her back and murmuring ineffectual words of comfort, when at last the shuddering sobs stilled to soft hiccups as she regained control.

'I'm sorry, Daisy, May...' She looked at them through blurred, swollen eyes. 'I didn't mean to inflict it all on you. It's just that...' She bit her lip as the tears threatened to overwhelm her again.

'It's not the master, is it?' Daisy suddenly had a look of horror straighten her round face. 'He hasn't taken advantage of you? You know—he hasn't...?'

'No, no, nothing like that.' Tania had to raise a weak smile at the look of maternal concern wobbling Daisy's red cheeks. 'It's too complicated to explain, but I really must leave. I can't see him again. Can I leave the rest of what he paid Mrs Jenkins with you to give him? Would you mind?'

'Of course not, dearie.' Daisy was dishing up a thick meaty stew as she spoke, setting a plateful in front of Tania with some crusty bread and putting a spoon into her trembling hand. 'But you're going to eat before you do anything else, and then we'll have a little talk. You look as though you're going to collapse at any moment, and I don't want that on my conscience.'

Tania had to admit that the food helped her feel more normal, and after she had cleared her plate and drunk two hot, sweet mugfuls of May's excessively strong tea, she felt a little of her old spirit beginning to take hold. She desperately needed to confide in someone, and the two women were so kind. She began to relate the whole sorry story as the wind howled and whined outside and sharp gusts of rain beat with ever-increasing fury against the old leaded windows.

'Well, it seems to me the first thing you need is somewhere to stay until you sort yourself out.' Tania was grateful they hadn't offered any opinion or judgement as she had finished talking. Good practical common sense was what she needed now, and she had the feeling she couldn't have come to a better place.

'There's no chance you will change your mind and stay?' Tania shook her head as Daisy asked the question. 'Well, then, I think we might have the answer to your problem, at least for a few weeks, that is.'

'You have?' Tania stared at the country woman in surprise, and Daisy laughed softly at the expression on her face.

'We had one of our old friends visit over Christmas. Mr Meliora said it would be all right.' Tania nodded. 'The poor soul was full of woe. It appears her son's wife has had to go into hospital for a few weeks, and Megan is looking after the children—three little ones under five, and twins of seven.'

Tania drew her breath through her teeth in sympathy, and Daisy grimaced sombrely. 'Exactly. She's finding it hard going, as she's nearing sixty and she lost her husband two years ago. It seems to me she'd be mighty glad of a pair of extra hands, although she wouldn't be able to pay you much. They aren't the sort of people

who usually have nannies.' She laughed at her little joke
and May wheezed along with her.

'Oh, Daisy, that would be fantastic, and I wouldn't
want to be paid anything. If I could just stay with her
and work for my keep until I get another job...' Her
voice trailed away. 'Could you ring her now?'

'I was just going to suggest it.'

Within three hours Megan's son had arrived to collect
her in his old battered van, loading all her belongings
into its cavernous depths, and thanking her over and
over again on the way home for her help. 'I knew it was
too much for me mam, but there's no one else to have
'em,' he said as they hurtled along the wet roads in the
creaking little van. 'She's getting on a bit and her legs
aren't what they were, you know how it is...'

It turned out that the Hutchin family was the best
thing that could have happened to Tania in the circumstances. Megan was a sprightly little woman with
iron-grey hair and bright button eyes, and although the
children were hard work they were well-behaved, good
little souls, who were clearly missing their mother and
family home. After a few days Tania felt as though she
had known them all for years, and the days were so busy
that she had no time to brood on the past weeks, falling
into bed at night, utterly exhausted and asleep as soon
as her head touched the pillow. Megan's small house was
crowded to overflowing with the younger children's cots
and all their clothes and toys, and Tania had been de-
signated a camp-bed in the corner of Megan's bedroom,
but she didn't mind. There was nothing to remind her
of her former life.

The worst time was mid-afternoon, when the older
children were at school and the little ones were having
their nap. Megan looked on the hour or two of peace

as an oasis in the desert, but Tania would find her mind being drawn to a tall dark figure in her memory, and would work desperately at anything to stop her thoughts from concentrating on the path they wanted to follow. She had made Daisy and May swear not to reveal her whereabouts to anyone for the time being until she had licked her wounds, although she doubted such a warning was necessary. There was no one who would be interested in finding her anyway, and she had written to her parents to inform them of her new address.

It was during this quiet hour one afternoon when she had been with Megan for two weeks that a sharp knock sounded at the small front door. Megan was asleep upstairs, worn out, and she had been writing to apply for a job in the crêche at the nearby hospital that Megan's son had told her about. His wife was coming home the next day and the children would be back with their parents at the weekend.

She opened the door quickly, hoping the noise hadn't woken the little ones, and then felt all the breath leave her body in a constricting gasp as her stunned eyes took in the big dark man standing in taut silence on the step outside. For a moment she thought her mind was playing tricks, and then he spoke, his voice as deep and rich as she remembered. 'Hello, Tania. It's taken me quite some time to find you.'

She put up a hand as though to ward him off, her face whitening as she took a step backwards into the small room. 'What do you want?' Her voice was no more than a whisper, forced through pale lips, and as his eyes registered her shock they narrowed into black slits.

'I want to talk to you. There are things we need to discuss.'

'No!' She went to shut the door but he moved swiftly, putting his foot in the closing space and forcing the door open again.

'Don't be silly, Tania.' The sound of her name on his lips caused her stomach muscles to flutter alarmingly. He was the only person who made it into a soft, seductive caress. 'I need to talk to you alone. Can you come to the car for a few minutes?'

She looked through the open doorway to see the sleek powerful machine crouching a few yards up the road, its shiny smooth shape incongruous in the poor area in which Megan lived. 'How did you find me?' She looked up into the dark face and saw he looked grey and tired, as though he hadn't slept in days. 'Did Daisy——?'

'No, Daisy didn't give you away.' His tone was dry. 'I could have cut her tongue out and made them walk on hot coals before either of them would have revealed where you were hidden. It was your parents.' She stared at him, wide-eyed. 'It took me some time to trace them, but when I did they very kindly offered the information. I presume you haven't told them about our... disagreement?'

'I told them I had finished my work with your family,' she said stiffly. 'Now, if you'll please leave——'

'I have no intention of leaving until I have spoken with you properly. Now, you can conduct our private business for the whole of this street to hear if you like; I really don't mind. However, if you wish to retain a little dignity I suggest you do as I say and come to my car.' She looked at the windows in the house opposite, where the curtains were flapping unashamedly, and noticed that the elderly widow two doors along had decided it was time to whiten her step.

'I'll get my coat.' Her voice was weary with resignation.

'You'd better inform someone that you are with me. I don't want a charge of kidnapping added to my other sins.'

She looked at him sharply. 'I'm not going anywhere with you; please understand that.'

'If you aren't in my car in sixty seconds I'm going to batter the door down and carry you out.' It wasn't a threat, but more in the nature of a promise. He turned and walked towards the car, his stride calm and measured and his back straight.

'You unfeeling monster...' She glared at him before running upstairs to leave a note for Megan and grabbing her coat on the way down. She reached the car with a second to spare.

'Right.' He started the engine as soon as she slid into her seat, and the big car purred into life with a soft growl. 'I'm not going to sit here on show. I intend to drive a short distance to a secluded spot where we can talk, just talk. All right?'

She nodded without looking at him. His big body in the heavy thick overcoat was just a touch away, and she had thought she would never see him again. Keep control, keep control. Her brain was hammering the words in her mind, but the familiar delicious smell of him was reaching out to her and causing her spine to tingle in anticipation. This was the man who hated her, who considered her less than nothing. Keep it in your mind, Tania, she said silently to herself as they left the small village and turned down a quiet country lane, where paper-thin layers of mist were winding lazily across the distant fields.

Her stomach came up into her mouth as he turned off the engine after pulling a short distance into a deserted picnic area, and sat staring out of the windscreen with his hands resting on the steering-wheel.

'Don't ever, ever leave me again.' The husky words brought her head snapping up so that her hair fell across her face in dark red waves and her eyes opened wide in disbelief. 'When I came home and found you gone... If you wanted revenge for the way I've treated you you've had it.' His knuckles were white as they gripped the wheel. 'I've seriously thought there were times when I was losing my mind over the last two weeks.'

'You told me to go...' As he turned to face her she saw such a deep anguish twisting the fine features that her heart stopped beating.

'I know.' He groaned and went to touch her and then drew back, banging his fists against the dashboard. 'Believe me, I know. But I didn't think you would leave that day. I nearly went mad when I came back and Gilda said you had left.' He looked at her face, in which confusion and pain were warring with shock.

'I love you, Tania. It might be too late, but I've got to say it anyway. I would never have believed that another human being could make me feel the way I've felt in the last few days. The pain was indescribable—dying would have been a sweet relief.' He shook his head slowly. 'For the first time I realised how Catalina had felt, why it had all been worth it for her. I would have sacrificed the rest of my life for one hour of holding you close and hearing you say you loved me.'

'Enrico——'

'No, let me say it all.' He turned to stare out of the windscreen again, his face white and his big shoulders hunched. 'Whatever you think of me now, I have to say

it all, make you understand. I've been such a bitter,
stupid fool, and I knew it all along. I've loved you from
the moment you faced me on that dark country road
when some young maniac had knocked you off your
bike. Such a tiny, angry little thing, almost throwing
yourself in front of that great lout to protect him from
me. I couldn't believe you were for real.' He ran a hand
over his face in the gesture she knew so well before he
continued.

'I was determined from that first day to see you
again—that's why I sent those damn roses—but I
couldn't admit to myself how you had affected me. I
had to cover it up, to make a joke of it all. Then the
next day, when you walked into that hotel room...' He
turned to face her, his dark eyes eloquent. 'I had a hard
job not to leap across the desk and take you right then
and there.'

'I don't believe you.' Her voice was a soft whisper as
she fought against what he was saying. It could all be a
cruel game, and she couldn't survive another rejection
from him.

'Why should you? I don't blame you. I can't explain
how I felt, Tania. I'm not used to baring my soul to
anyone.'

'Try.'

He looked at her, a dark red flush turning his cheekbones into bronze. 'Do you know, I blessed that accident of mine because it forced you into my home? Oh,
I know you came because you felt guilty, and I could so
easily have let you off the hook, but I didn't want to. I
wanted you there with me, even though it was a mad
kind of torture. It was worse when I knew how you felt.
I had the opportunity to grasp heaven by the fingertips
and yet I couldn't. I couldn't.' He groaned and it sounded

like a wounded animal. 'To take the risk of loving someone the way Catalina had loved me—it was unthinkable, abhorrent. I couldn't willingly give so much power to any woman.'

She looked at him wonderingly as a tentative hope started deep inside her. 'What changed your mind?'

'Because when I saw you with Camillo, when I thought you had betrayed how I felt about you, I wanted to kill you both and then myself. My life finished at that moment.' He turned his face away from her. 'And later, even before Camillo explained what had really happened and how you had told him you loved me, I decided that I had to have you, no matter what. Even if it meant buying a desert island somewhere and moving there so you never got the chance to meet another man.' His voice was shaking. 'I couldn't face the rest of my life without you and I can't now. If you tell me I've killed your love for me——'

'You couldn't do that,' she whispered softly. 'Oh, my darling...' As she fell against him his arms went round her in a hug that stopped her breathing, and he was kissing the glittering tears that were flooding down her face.

'Don't cry.' His voice was cracked. 'I never want to make you cry again. I'll spend the rest of my life making you happy. You are all I want.' He strained her to him in an agony of desire. 'Whatever you want will be yours.'

'I've only ever wanted you.'

He looked deep into her starry eyes, letting her see the love he had kept hidden for so long. 'You'll marry me soon?'

'It can't be soon enough.'

'Shameless wench.' His voice was trembling as his lips burnt a frantic trail over her upturned face. 'I've never really been married before, my darling, only with this.' He touched his body. 'Never with this.' He placed her hand on his heart. 'I shall never let you go, and I'm not easy to live with.'

'You told me before. I don't care.'

As he drew her into him she shivered, feeling the evidence of his passion hard and strong against the softness of her body. 'We are going to make beautiful *bambini*, my little English hedgehog.'

He was stroking her body through the thin silk of her blouse, and she was lost in the feel and smell of him, her breath coming in tiny panting sobs against the hard tanned skin of his face. 'I'm going to love you every day of my life until you beg me to stop.'

For an answer she pulled his face down to hers and covered his mouth in a long, lingering kiss.

'Stop talking, Enrico.'

He did; the language of love said it all.

Next Month's Romances

Each month you can choose from a world of variety in romance with Mills & Boon. Below are the new titles to look out for next month, why not ask either Mills & Boon Reader Service or your Newsagent to reserve you a copy of the titles you want to buy — just tick the titles you would like to order and either post to Reader Service or take it to any Newsagent and ask them to order your books.

Please save me the following titles:	Please tick	√
PAST LOVING	Penny Jordan	
WINTER OF DREAMS	Susan Napier	
KNIGHT TO THE RESCUE	Miranda Lee	
OUT OF NOWHERE	Patricia Wilson	
SECOND CHANCE FOR LOVE	Susanne McCarthy	
MORE THAN A DREAM	Emma Richmond	
REVENGE	Natalie Fox	
YESTERDAY AND FOREVER	Sandra Marton	
NO GENTLEMAN	Kate Walker	
CATALINA'S LOVER	Vanessa Grant	
OLD LOVE, NEW LOVE	Jennifer Taylor	
A FRENCH ENCOUNTER	Cathy Williams	
THE TRESPASSER	Jane Donnelly	
A TEMPTING SHORE	Dana James	
A LOVE TO LAST	Samantha Day	
A PLACE OF WILD HONEY	Ann Charlton	

If you would like to order these books from Mills & Boon Reader Service please send £1.70 per title to: Mills & Boon Reader Service, P.O. Box 236, Croydon, Surrey, CR9 3RU and quote your Subscriber No:...(If applicable) and complete the name and address details below. Alternatively, these books are available from many local Newsagents including W.H.Smith, J.Menzies, Martins and other paperback stockists from 14th August 1992.

Name:..

Address:..

....Post Code:.......................

To Retailer: If you would like to stock M&B books please contact your regular book/magazine wholesaler for details.

You may be mailed with offers from other reputable companies as a result of this application. If you would rather not take advantage of these opportunities please tick box ☐

SOMETHING OLD,
SOMETHING NEW,
SOMETHING BORROWED,
SOMETHING BLUE

Four short stories all featuring one aspect of this
traditional wedding rhyme have been specially
commissioned from four bestselling authors and
presented in one attractive volume for you to enjoy.

SOMETHING OLD
Mary Lyons

SOMETHING NEW
Valerie Parv

**SOMETHING
BORROWED**
Miranda Lee

SOMETHING BLUE
Emma Goldrick

Available July 1992
Price: £3.99

4 FREE

Romances
and 2 FREE gifts
just for you!

*You can enjoy all the
heartwarming emotion of true love for FREE!
Discover the heartbreak and the happiness, the emotion and
the tenderness of the modern relationships in
Mills & Boon Romances.*

*We'll send you 4 captivating Romances as a special offer from
Mills & Boon Reader Service, along with the chance to have
6 Romances delivered to your door each month.*

Claim your FREE books and gifts overleaf...

An irresistible offer from Mills & Boon

Here's a personal invitation from Mills & Boon Reader Service, to become a regular reader of Romances. To welcome you, we'd like you to have 4 books, a CUDDLY TEDDY and a special MYSTERY GIFT absolutely FREE.

Then you could look forward each month to receiving 6 brand new Romances, delivered to your door, postage and packing free! Plus our free Newsletter featuring author news, competitions, special offers and much more.

This invitation comes with no strings attached. You may cancel or suspend your subscription at any time, and still keep your free books and gifts.

It's so easy. Send no money now. Simply fill in the coupon below and post it to -
Reader Service, FREEPOST,
PO Box 236, Croydon, Surrey CR9 9EL.

NO STAMP REQUIRED

Free Books Coupon

Yes! Please rush me 4 free Romances and 2 free gifts! Please also reserve me a Reader Service subscription. If I decide to subscribe I can look forward to receiving 6 brand new Romances each month for just £10.20, postage and packing free. If I choose not to subscribe I shall write to you within 10 days - I can keep the books and gifts whatever I decide. I may cancel or suspend my subscription at any time. I am over 18 years of age.

Ms/Mrs/Miss/Mr_____ EP31R

Address _____

_____

Postcode_____Signature _____